DANGEROUS JOURNEY

DANGEROUS JOURNEY

JOANNE PENCE

QUAIL HILL PUBLISHING

Quail Hill Publishing

PO Box 64

Eagle, ID 83616

First e-book edition: May 2012

Second e-book edition: September 2012

First Quail Hill Publishing Print Book: April 2017

Second Quail Hill Publishing Print Book: August 2018

ISBN: 978-1-949566-14-7

DANGEROUS JOURNEY

CHAPTER 1

$\mathcal{H}$ong Kong, British Crown Colony, 1978

"You call yourselves police? What do you mean you still haven't heard anything about my brother?"

"Look, Miss…uh, Perkins." The balding, ruddy-faced policeman slowly lifted his gaze from the newspaper on the counter and wiped the perspiration from his brow with a once-white handkerchief. "We are trying to be sympathetic, we are trying to be reasonable," he droned, "but each year, hundreds of American tourists show up to peer from the Hong Kong border into the heart of Mao's China, or to actually enter it in their well-guarded little tour groups. You simply cannot expect us to remember one individual. Good day, Miss Perkins."

C.J. Perkins folded her arms, one toe tapping as she glared at the man immersed once again in the latest round of tabloid scandals.

Until a few days ago, everything C.J. knew about Hong Kong came from old movies like *The World of Suzie Wong* and *Love is a Many Splendored Thing* which she'd shed many a tear over. But they didn't prepare her for the real place. She learned that the Hong Kong British Crown Colony was made up of several parts: the island of Hong Kong, the mainland city called Kowloon, and to the north, the area called the New Territories. They were separated from Communist China by a well-patrolled border. Already, there was much talk and nervousness in Hong Kong about the British lease running out in another ten years, and that the colony would revert to the People's Republic of China. No one could believe that would ever happen, however.

Now, C.J. found herself in the town of Luchow deep in the New Territories and near the Chinese border. As opposed to the modern, high-rise filled Hong Kong and Kowloon areas, the New Territories were old, comparatively barren, ramshackle and laden with yellow dust.

At midday the Luchow police station was quiet, the heat and humidity high enough to keep troublemakers comfortably indoors and the border town relatively crime-free. Only the rhythmic whirring of the ceiling fans and the patter of insects hitting the window screens broke the soporific silence.

The policeman raised one eye in her direction, a look of disdain on his face, and returned to his reading.

Frowning, she remained where she was, waiting for him to do something. Anything. Hot and tired, she angrily shoved a frizzy, humidity-crinkled lock of brown hair behind her ear. Her frustration soared at the heat-induced lethargy surrounding her.

There was only one way to deal with these people, she decided. After all, her brother was missing. She had tried sweetness, patience and understanding, and had gotten nowhere. She hadn't tried to be flirtatious. She was well aware she wasn't the type to pull that off.

It was time to be tough.

She linked her thumbs in the belt loops of her white cotton slacks and squared her shoulders under her red plaid blouse. She spread her feet apart, the small stacked heels of her white sandals adding two inches to an already tall frame, and took a deep breath.

"I am an American citizen." Her voice was low, well-modulated and controlled as she spoke, even though she knew her statement didn't mean as much throughout Asia as it had before the recent pull-out from Vietnam. She continued. "My brother, Alan Mansfred Perkins, has been missing for three weeks, his papers show that he planned to come here, and now, he's disappeared." When the officer still didn't move, her fury boiled over. "I demand that you do something!"

He looked up, his eyes half-closed. "So you've told us, over and over. But you still haven't told us why. Why did he want to come to Luchow? What was his reason?"

The same unanswerable questions again and again, she thought, as her fists clenched. "I'm not a mind-reader! I don't know! I don't care!"

He slammed his hand on the counter and pushed his round, pugnacious face toward hers. "Well, neither do I! And he's *your* brother!"

"He's *your* missing person! I want you to try to find him!"

"If he shows up, we'll let you know."

His breath was hot and smelled revolting. C.J. spun around hugging her arms, her cheeks burning and her chest heaving. This was the same annoying claptrap she had received for days. And she was still no closer to finding Alan.

She shut her eyes for a moment as a wave of despair and worry filled her, but she fought against it and turned again to face the epitome of bureaucratic implacability. "I must speak with your chief."

"I'm sorry," he said, although he sounded quite the opposite. "He's away at the moment, and I've no idea when he will return."

"May I wait?"

"My pleasure." His sarcasm dripped as he left the front desk to shuffle papers elsewhere in the room.

C.J. stubbornly plopped down on the old vinyl-covered sofa across from the counter, causing puffs of dust and the scent of mildew to waft up to her. She picked up a Chinese magazine and briskly fanned herself against the sweltering heat. Her blouse kept sticking to the plastic furniture.

Where was the police chief? She looked around the station she had come to know well—too well— over the past few days. The large main room, its plaster walls cracked and gray with age, was empty, as usual. So were the chief's office and some small rooms beside it. On the far end of the main office was the door to the jail cells, which were about the only part of the station she hadn't seen yet. She had no desire to change that.

Over an hour passed, but still the police chief did not return. C.J. willed herself to be patient and leaned back on the sofa with a weary sigh. That she had nowhere else to go and had reached the end of her brother's miniscule trail, made her resolution to remain here easy to keep. She also had a niggling feeling that the police were hiding something from her, and she was determined to stay until she found out what it was.

As the heat and humidity of the afternoon made the air thicker and more oppressive, even the ceiling fans seemed to slacken their pace. She put down the magazine to concentrate on making no movement whatsoever. Her eyelids grew heavy, and her thoughts drifted freely....

If she were to go home now, what could she tell her parents? That she almost found Alan, but not quite? That she had failed again? Just as she had with her career? Her art work?

Her parents had paid for art school for her to become the "female Rembrandt of her time." But the main lesson she had learned, much to her own dismay, was that even dedication and hard work don't always result in truly creative talent. Not that she was untalented, she just wasn't a great artist. Her work was technically competent, well-executed and likable. But nothing more. . . nothing more...

Her eyelids flew open. She must have fallen asleep, she thought, as she quickly pulled herself upright on the old sofa and wondered if anyone had noticed. Mercifully, the office appeared empty. So why had she awakened so suddenly?

"What are you doing in Luchow?"

The voice startled her so badly she nearly toppled off the couch. It belonged to Captain Burnham of the British border patrol, a memorably odious person. Tall and heavy, with a florid complexion and thinning dirty blond hair, he could have stepped out of a 1940s movie about the Third Reich, except for his very British accent.

"I wish to speak to the American Consul." A deep, male voice with a pure Yankee twang to it answered Burnham.

After days of unhelpful British accents, the resonant sound was comforting to her homesick ears. The voices came from one of the small rooms off the main office, but she couldn't see anyone.

"What are you doing here?" the captain repeated.

The American gave the same response.

"You'll go to the consulate in good time, after you answer our questions. Now, where are your papers?"

"I wish to see the American Consul."

The voices grew louder.

"Were you in Communist China?"

"I wish to see—"

"Tell us your name."

"I wish—"

"I want your name!"

"I wish to see—"

"Does the name Alan Perkins mean anything to you?"

At this, C.J. froze, every sense alert. Who was this man? Why would Burnham ask him about her brother? She heard his standard reply and felt as irritated by it as she suspected Burnham did.

"Tell us about the White Dragon," Captain Burnham said.

C.J. all but gasped aloud, and covered her mouth with her hands.

The White Dragon was the name she had found on a note in Alan's room—the same note that had led her to Hong Kong. She had asked the police about it over and over, but they had consistently maintained that they had no idea what it was. Now she knew that it did mean something to them. They had lied to her! But why?

"...American Consul." The last words of the man's pat answer drummed once again in her ears. She jumped up and moved closer to the back room, throwing herself against the counter that blocked her way as she strained to hear every word.

"Lock him up," Burnham said.

No! Her mind spun. *They can't do that!*

Since the border patrol was asking the stranger about Alan and the White Dragon, he must know something. He wouldn't tell them, but maybe he would tell her, a fellow American. He had to tell her! He was her only lead.

She chewed her bottom lip, uncertain what to do or how to find a way to talk to the stranger.

She was still considering her options when she heard a slight shuffling sound; then a tall, thin man was pushed into the large office from the small side room. He stumbled once before he regained his footing. He wasn't merely being questioned. To her dismay, she saw that he was handcuffed. He was a prisoner.

His jeans and dark green T-shirt were torn, and layers of dirt clung to his clothes, face and arms. Yet, despite the handcuffs at his back, he held his spine straight and his head erect.

His long, sun-bleached, light brown hair was pushed straight back from his forehead. His face was bearded with prominent cheekbones, a patrician nose and high forehead. A jagged scar cut across his left eyebrow, and his skin was deeply bronzed by the sun.

The defiant look he wore made her think that capturing him had probably not been one of the border patrol's easier missions. Considering how she felt about the authorities in Luchow, the thought gave her perverse pleasure.

She took a step forward. He raised his eyes to hers, and their glances met across the large room.

His eyes were a startling green. She had seen that exact shade in the jungles of Malaysia where her brother had last been living, on the uppermost leaves of the rain forest when it was flooded in sunlight. As she felt herself ensnared within their depths, they reminded her further of the jungle—beautiful, yet frightening; enticing, yet threatening.

She hadn't meant to stare, hadn't meant to lock her gaze with his, but was unable to break away.

A slightly questioning look flickered across his face for a moment; then he gave a rakish grin and turned again toward the captain. The grin startled her at first, but then she realized that it had only added to the self-assured demeanor of the man. He had the look of a feline playing with its prey. He was, in a word, magnificent.

In that same instant, she knew what he saw when he looked at her, and why, far too suddenly, he had turned away. She was a woman who was "a little too"—a little too tall, a little too clumsy, and, she had to admit, a little too bossy. Her hair was too mousy-brown to be pretty, and styled too simply--shoulder length with a side part--to be chic. Her mouth was too big, and her eyes too pale a gray. She was, in a word, plain. Being able to captivate a man with her beauty wasn't her long suit. Not even when the man was already a prisoner. That knowledge didn't make approaching him any easier, but she had to find a way to speak to him. As she studied him, a plan formed. He didn't seem like a criminal, she thought. Or not quite. And the authorities were so hopeless. Dare she chance it? If it failed, what was the worst that could happen to her?

She didn't want to contemplate the answer.

Okay, C period, J period, Perkins. You've always said you're tough—now's your chance to prove it.

She swallowed hard as she braced herself to take the plunge. She bolted around the counter and across the room. "Wait!" she shouted.

The men turned to look at her.

"You found him!" she cried. "You found my brother!"

She stopped in front of the prisoner and put her hands on his arms. "Alan! Thank God! We were so worried."

He accepted her greeting without the slightest twitch, although her own body was trembling so badly that she was convinced she would give herself away. Understand, her eyes pleaded with him. Please understand! Putting her shaking arms around him, she pulled his head against the side of her face. He stiffened at first, then bent toward her without complaint.

She patted his back with sisterly affection. "Oh, poor Alan. What happened to you out there? It must have been terrible. Don't worry, I'm here now to take care of you. I've got your papers, and we'll be home in Columbus in no time." She knew she was babbling, but couldn't stop. "Mom and Dad have been so worried."

He straightened and stared at her. As she stroked his hair back from his face, her eyes met his. The power his gaze had exercised over her from across the room was insignificant compared to this, and her hand faltered, then dropped to her side as her stomach did a triple somersault.

She tore her gaze from him to the captain, forcing a smile. "I don't know how to thank you," she said.

Burnham's eyes narrowed as his head snapped from one to the other. "This is your brother?" Incredulity dripped from his voice.

"He must have been robbed and beaten. That's obviously why he looks this way," she said. The stranger lifted one eyebrow at her.

She began to pat his shoulder, hoping to distract him from protesting, hoping to signal her distress, and praying for him to go along with her.

"Let me see his papers again," the captain said.

She handed over the identification papers she had found in Alan's room in Malaysia. His passport, however, was not among them.

"Six feet tall, two hundred pounds, dark brown hair, brown eyes," Burnham read, then eyed his prisoner as he rubbed his hand against his chin. "Six-two, I would say. Twelve, thirteen stone, at most—that's a hundred seventy or so pounds to you," he said to C.J. "Hair is brown, sort of. But the eyes..."

She felt flustered. The prisoner cocked his head at her with "Now what?" on his face. She raised her chin. "So he lost weight in this godforsaken part of the world! Who wouldn't?" That was when she noticed that the captain's stomach stood quite a bit nearer to her than did his feet.

She grabbed Alan's papers from Burnham's hands and stuffed them quickly back into her purse, her words tumbling out ever faster. "You know men don't worry about little things like inches. They're all six-footers or they're short, that's all. There's no other height they worry about. And his eyes, I ask you, how many men really think about the color of their eyes? I'm sure ninety percent of the men in the world say their eyes are brown."

"Ninety percent of the men in the world *do* have brown eyes."

"My point exactly, so what's a little—"

The prisoner stepped forward. "If these are my papers and she is my sister, then what charge am I being held on?"

C.J.'s mouth fell open; she couldn't believe the authority in the man's voice. Even Burnham looked surprised.

"*If* those are your papers, there is no charge at the moment. Not from us, in any case. If you are, in fact, Alan Perkins and this is your sister, you have far greater problems than the border patrol could provide." Burnham scowled. "And there are still some questions—"

"And I told you, I have no answers. Now, I suggest you remove these handcuffs and let me out of here, or you'll be facing a false arrest charge."

C.J. got ready to run when she saw the rage slowly well up in Burnham's face and threaten to explode at any second. "I suggest you both leave Luchow immediately, and that you do not return. I have enough trouble with Chinese Communists just across the border. I don't need more from you Americans."

"What would the free world do without you?" the prisoner said as his handcuffs were removed and his bedroll was handed to him. As C.J. stood bewildered by all this, he clasped her elbow. Before she knew it, she was standing on the street outside the station.

The busy street was narrow and lined with small shops displaying all manner of edibles and household necessities, a crush of people went about their business. Some were dressed western style, while many wore loose fitting pants and tunic tops. Shoppers haggled over prices, mothers disciplined wayward offspring, radios blared the latest Cantonese tunes, and cars, carts and animals all added to the cacophony of sound that greeted C.J. as she stood there, unsure what she should do next. Dust flew everywhere and the strong smells of roasted and fried foods, ginger, garlic and soy hung in the air.

In the midst of this, the stranger took her hand and kissed the back of it, his eyes bright. "Thank you, fair damsel. You're a friend indeed. Goodbye." He turned smoothly and started walking down the street.

Goodbye? She stood immobile as she watched him melt into the sea of pedestrians. "Wait!"

He neither stopped nor slowed down, simply continued to ease his way through the thick crowd as if he belonged there. C.J. had to struggle, and felt almost rude as she pushed her way through the mass of people who were as unwavering in their purpose as she was in hers.

Finally she reached him, but he barely glanced at her.

"Wait! I need your help," she cried. "I didn't get you out of there for nothing!"

"I know. Your brother, Alan Perkins."

"You know him?"

"I know of him."

"You do? That's more than the police will admit to," she said bitterly. "You've got to help me find him."

"No, I don't."

"I have nowhere else to turn."

"You mean nothing to me but trouble."

"Trouble?" What could he mean? She was the one who'd gotten him out of trouble.

He hurried on.

She ran to catch up. "Please." Her voice cracked; she was close to tears. Chasing a man down the street wasn't a usual part of her routine.

A look of weariness came over him. He sighed, and turning to her, looked her straight in the eye. "I'd like to find your brother, too. In fact, a lot of people would. But it's just not worth it to me. And it's not the kind of thing for a woman to get mixed up in. Do you understand?"

All the worry and frustration she had felt for a whole week welled up in her. "What do you mean not the kind of thing for a woman? It's my brother we're talking about! Whatever's going on, I'm already

mixed up in it—the 'blood' kind of mixed up. I care. Can't you understand that? I love him."

He regarded her a long moment before continuing on his way.

Embarrassed, she wiped away the angry tears that trickled down
her cheeks, then ran and caught his arm, refusing to release it until he
spun angrily in her direction. "Why won't you tell me what you
know?" she demanded. "Why won't you help me? Haven't you ever
had a brother—or someone—you cared about so much you'd do
anything for them? Haven't you?"

His eyes darkened. "Once," he replied, his voice low and harsh.

Something in his look made her drop her hand. He paused
momentarily, then continued walking. She dogged his steps. The
crowds thinned as they left the busiest part of the colorful market-
place. She had no idea where they were going. He's so obstinate, she
thought; he even looks obstinate. How could I have thought him
handsome?

His face was an intriguing mixture, though. His eyes were
surrounded by dark hollows and deeply set. His profile reminded her
of engravings she had seen of Roman emperors on old coins, but at
the same time, there was a ruggedness about him.

She glanced at him again and noticed his wariness, a sense that he
was alert to everything nearby and could strike like a rattlesnake at
any hint of danger. She shuddered slightly.

"Cold?" he asked, his voice surprisingly gentle.

"No. I was just wondering how the police managed to pick you up.
I wouldn't have thought it possible for them to catch anyone." Least
of all you, she added silently.

He looked at her quizzically. "You don't have a very good impression of the police here, do you? Anyway, it was the border patrol,
Burnham's group, that picked me up. Not that that's any justification.
It was my own fault. I was too tired. A man makes mistakes at
such times."

"You were arrested because you had no papers?"

"Apparently."

"But why?"

"Must have misplaced them."

"I see." She gulped, realizing she didn't see at all, and that she
might not *want* to see.

"Where are you staying?" she asked, realizing that she still had to talk to him, no matter what.

"Nowhere."

"I have a car. I can drive you wherever you want to go."

"I haven't decided."

"Look, I really must—"

"Go home." He turned a corner.

She turned as well. "I won't give up, and I won't let you simply disappear on me!"

He nodded wearily. "I seem to be getting that message."

"I've told the police you're my brother! I'm responsible. What if Burnham comes to find—"

The look he gave her stopped her. They both knew that wasn't the point.

She gritted her teeth. The man did look ready to drop with exhaustion. "If you need to rest, I've got a room."

"Oh?" His right eyebrow rose ever so slightly as his glance swept appraisingly over her body. A dangerous man all right, she thought.

"I'm only talking about a little while! Just long enough for you to lie down, I mean…um…take a nap." There was no way she could make it sound right.

"Nap?" His incredulous expression told her that he probably hadn't heard that word since kindergarten.

She tried to ignore the warm rush of color that filled her cheeks as she continued, desperation spurring her on. "You can get something to eat, too. You must be hungry. And after that we can talk. Look, there'll be no need to worry about the police, or, or anything. Just eat, sleep, and then tell me what you know about Alan. Okay?" She paused, hoping against hope that he wouldn't object.

"Come with me," she continued when he didn't reply. "My room's not here in Luchow; it's on the edge of Kowloon. I'll drive, and we'll be there in no time at all."

His steps slowed, as if by allowing himself to think about the needs of his body, the energy he had called upon earlier vanished.

"It's got a nice, soft bed," she added, "with fluffy down pillows."

"Is it a double?"

"I thought you were tired! Best of all, it has a bath with hot, running water."

"You win." He stopped walking, looking as if he could barely take another step. "Which way is heaven?"

CHAPTER 2

C.J. unlocked the door to the passenger side of the rented white Toyota. The stranger climbed in while she went around to the driver's side.

She glanced at him as she started the engine and slowly eased the car into traffic. Already, he had dropped his head against the headrest, his eyes shut.

Finally she had found someone who had information about Alan. The anticipation of what she might learn was hard to bear. Perhaps soon this whole mad episode would be over and she could return home.

Thoughts of all that had happened in the two weeks since she had received the bizarre phone call from her mother came rushing back at her. Since then, she had seen and done things she couldn't have imagined before, had found herself in places she hadn't even known existed. The recollection made her shudder.

Her brother was a Peace Corps volunteer. After the Vietnam War, Watergate, and the recessions under Presidents Nixon, Ford and now Carter, Alan had given up on finding a good job in the U.S. and took off for Sarawak, a part of Malaysia on the South China Sea. When her parents received a telegram that he hadn't returned from leave as expected, they telephoned C.J. from their home in Columbus, Ohio.

C.J. had known something was wrong as soon as she heard her

mother's voice. Mildred Perkins saw the idea of making a telephone call to Los Angeles as purely frivolous. Letters had worked well enough for her Puritan forefathers, after all. "A penny saved is a penny earned," was Mildred's favorite expression, and one that C.J. did her best to ignore.

Her mother had told her that it would be wisest if she were the one to go to Malaysia to find out what had happened to Alan, since her father had a "delicate constitution." Of course, the family would pay the whole bill, knowing C.J. hardly had enough money to make ends meet. That was her fault, Mildred reminded her, for not having a real job.

"You don't think those heathen cannibals got him, do you, C.J.?" Mildred had asked, a familiar note of pious indignation in her voice.

C.J. had cringed. "I really doubt Alan's ended up in a stew pot, Mother. If he were hurt, I'm sure we'd have heard something."

"This is no time for levity!"

"Goodbye, Mother. I'll write when I find out what's going on with Alan."

"C.J., wait. Your father and I are so anxious....Send us a telegram when you learn something. Goodbye, dear."

C.J. hung up the phone, then stood looking at it with dismay. What would her mother do without her?

Her father, Charles, was a dreamer, and Alan was just like him. Mildred was forever sheltering both of them from life's difficulties. With Mildred so busy seeing to her men, it always fell to C.J. to actually straighten out any dilemmas that arose. Her move to Los Angeles five years ago, at age twenty-three, had been her escape from that burden. Not that it had turned out exactly as she had hoped, but at least she was on her own.

But now, once again, she was being asked to solve a family problem. She was firmly convinced that Alan's so-called disappearance could be explained easily. He was thirty-one years old, after all, and didn't have to account for his every move.

As the thought of a journey to Southeast Asia had become more real to her, she rather selfishly hoped it could be turned into at least a little adventure while she was there.

Once she had gotten off the phone with her mother, she began making a mental checklist of everything she had to do before her trip.

Thanks to a ten-day bus tour through France, her passport was current so she only had to obtain emergency visas.

Two days after Mildred's call, C.J. was on a plane to Singapore, a flight of over twenty hours, followed by another full day to Sarawak on the island of Borneo. Once there, she hired a driver to take her to the small village of Bir Sakan, where Alan had been assigned.

C.J. hadn't ever heard of Sarawak before Alan was sent there. She had heard of Borneo only because old movies and even older circuses used to refer to "wild men of Borneo." She had no idea who or what they were.

She quickly learned that the island of Borneo was uncultivated except for a few locations along the ocean and major rivers. Beyond them was pure jungle. Who or what inhabited that jungle was anyone's guess—but headhunters definitely lived out there once upon a time.

In Bir Sakan, C.J. learned that Alan had supposedly gone to Singapore because of an "emergency in the family," and when he didn't return after three weeks, his fellow Peace Corpsmen had become concerned. Rumors persisted of his having been sighted elsewhere on the island, but a search had turned up no trace of him. He had disappeared.

C.J. had been confident that, once she got to Sarawak she would straighten everything out. After all, nothing ever happened to her or Alan that was either interesting or worth worrying about.

Not until she arrived at the small village on the edge of a frightening, mysterious jungle did she face up to the grim possibilities of what might have happened.

Alan's tiny room hadn't been touched since he left. C.J. searched his belongings for some clue to his whereabouts, but everything seemed to be there except for his passport. Other identification papers were neatly placed in a drawer. She took them out and put them in her purse. There were no pictures. She found nothing else, until she began rummaging in a large can that doubled as a wastebasket. There, amidst some candy bar wrappers were tiny scraps of paper. She scooped them up and placed them on the desk, fitting the pieces together like a jigsaw puzzle, and then taping them. She studied the result and wondered what its significance could be.

"Luchow," "HK," and "Bai-loong" were written in Roman letters, and beneath them were two Chinese characters. No one in Bir Sakan knew the meaning of the note.

C.J. stayed in the village one more day talking to people and poking about in Alan's belongings. After that, she flew back to Singapore to go to the American Consulate. She introduced herself, explained that she needed a translator, and was led to the office of a Chinese gentleman.

"Can you tell me the meaning of 'Luchow,' 'HK,' and 'Bai-loong'?" she asked, wasting not one second on pleasantries or small talk.

The man looked at her curiously. "Well. . ." He hesitated, as if considering the possibilities. "In this part of the world, 'HK' means only one thing—Hong Kong, the British Crown Colony. And Luchow is a small town in the New Territories portion of the Crown Colony, near the border with the People's Republic of China."

C.J. nodded, her fingers tapping her lips in thought. A town on the Chinese border...so that explained Luchow and HK. But what about the other word? "What does 'Bai-loong' mean to you?" she asked.

He shook his head and appeared perplexed.

"Here." She took Alan's paper with the Chinese characters from her wallet and handed it to him. "Maybe this will help."

His brow furrowed with concentration as he glanced at the paper. "It says 'white dragon.'"

"What does that mean?"

With a shrug, he handed the paper back to her, his face expressionless once again. "Who knows? It might be nothing more than the name of a restaurant. I'm sorry, Miss Perkins."

At that he bowed and turned back to his desk; the interview had ended. Irritated, C.J. marched out of the office. A restaurant indeed!

Standing outside the consulate, she pondered her options and made a decision. She caught a taxi to the airport and booked passage on the next available flight to Hong Kong.

When she arrived at Hong Kong's Kai Tak International Airport, she was physically and emotionally exhausted. Her task seemed increasingly hopeless. She stumbled from the plane into a taxi and asked to be taken to the nearest cheap hotel.

The next day, she rented a car and began a week's worth of frustration. Again and again she was given the same answer. On Hong Kong Island, on Kowloon, in Luchow. From the police, from the immigration authorities, from both American and Malaysian consulates. No matter where or to whom she spoke, she received the same response: We know nothing of your brother.

She had lost all hope until the arrival of the arrogant stranger she had "rescued" from the clutches of the border patrol—the man who was now sleeping peacefully beside her as she drove.

She hadn't even thought to ask his name.

CHAPTER 3

"My brother, Alan, will be joining me in my room for a short while," C.J. told the desk clerk, "If there is any additional cost, just add it to my bill, please."

The clerk looked up from the racing form he had been studying, his black eyes darting from. C.J. to the man beside her. His mouth grew pinched as his gaze swept over the man's grubby appearance. "Your…brother." He didn't believe her for a minute, and bent over the tout sheets again. "To each his own," he muttered.

C.J. gave the top of his head a scathing glare.

She and the stranger rode the elevator to the fourth floor, and entered her room. It wasn't very large to start with, and with this man inside it seemed infinitesimal. The room was cheap but clean, painted a gaudy robin's egg blue, with garish floral drapery and a green chenille bedspread on the double bed. A chest of drawers, a small writing desk and two wooden chairs completed the furnishings.

C.J. opened the window, feeling the need to do whatever she could to make the area seem more spacious. The window looked out over a courtyard filled with trash cans and bundles of old newspapers.

The man dropped his bedroll in the corner, his face impassive. "This isn't a tourist hotel. How did you find it?" he asked.

"A taxi driver." She wondered if she should start to quiz him about Alan yet.

He crossed the room to the window in two strides and leaned out, quickly glancing down, up and to the sides, then withdrew and seemed to relax. Peering at his grubby outfit, he frowned. "If you don't mind, the thought of a bath…"

"Please," she said quickly. "Be my guest."

He nodded and went into the bathroom.

She sank onto a chair, her elbows on her knees, and her head in her hands. *Oh, C.J.,* she thought. *What have you done now?*

But almost immediately, Mildred's long years of training on the care of others came rushing back to her as, hesitantly, she approached the bathroom door.

"Excuse me," she called over the sound of water running into the tub.

"Yes?"

"If you just toss your clothes out, I'll send them to be laundered. They do a quick job here."

"Great. There's some more stuff in the bedroll, if you don't mind."

"Oh? Well, sure."

"Also, I have a razor with my clothes. I forgot to grab it. If you could hand it to me?"

"No problem."

"And shaving cream. I don't have any. Do you think you could call room—"

"Yes!" My God, she thought, have I created a monster?

He opened the door slightly and handed her his clothes.

She tried not to face him as she took them, then opened up his bedroll to get the others.

She called room service, ordering dinner and shaving cream, and sent the stranger's clothes out to be cleaned. As soon as she heard the water stop running and the slight sloshing as he got in, she returned to the bedroll. In it were his few possessions: a wallet, a pocket knife, a razor and one key. She inspected the wallet, trying to find some clue as to who he was. There was nothing, not one piece of identification. She shook it out.

Still nothing.

About fifteen minutes later, a light tap at her door meant dinner. The bellboy looked with curiosity at the mess filling the room as he put down the tray.

C.J. set the dinner dishes on the small writing table, placed a chair on each side, then sat and waited for the stranger to emerge. Five minutes of silence later, she began to worry.

She knocked at the door. "Are you all right?"

"Wonderful. This is great! Want to join me?"

She jumped back, glad he couldn't see the blush lighting up her cheeks at the picture her overly active imagination had conjured up.

"Dinner's here. You don't want it to get cold," she said, deciding it was best just to ignore his question.

"Dinner? That's the one word you could say that would get me out of here. Be with you in a minute."

A short while later he joined her, a thick white bath towel secured around his waist, his chest and legs bare, his face freshly shaved, and his hair glistening. He had a good build, with broad, muscular shoulders tapering to a narrow waist and hips. With the beard and mustache gone, she noticed that his face was more rugged than she had expected, but it didn't detract from his attractiveness at all. If anything, it added to it. Her artist's eye had suspected there was a good-looking man under all that dirt, and she had been right. She felt her temperature go up at least five degrees.

"Sorry about the towel. I travel light," he said. "Unless you've got a robe I could borrow?"

She gave what she hoped was a saucy little toss of the head. "No bathrobe in your bedroll? Whatever would Miss Manners say? Your clothes should be returned soon. Come on, let's eat."

She took the tops off the bowls of Cantonese *war won ton*, walnut chicken in black bean sauce, bok choy with beef, pork chow mein and rice. He didn't load up his plate, but ate Chinese style, putting bits of food onto his rice bowl with his chopsticks. As he ate, C.J. noticed several long scars interrupting the smoothly tanned skin of one forearm and wondered what outrageous undertaking he had been involved in to get those. They reminded her once again how little she knew about him, and that she needed to be careful.

As she picked at her food, she watched with growing wonder as he polished off one dish after another. She thought she had ordered far too much, since she hadn't been sure which dishes he would like, but now she was afraid she hadn't ordered enough.

Finally he sat back and placed his bands on his stomach, his green eyes shining. "I think I've injured myself," he groaned.

What? "I'm sorry—"

"No, it's wonderful." His smile was lazy. "I haven't eaten this much since. . . Rangoon? Right, it was Rangoon. Two, three months ago."

She sat looking at him, not knowing what to do or say. He offered no assistance, and the silence grew. "Would you like some coffee? Cigarettes? Anything?" she asked finally.

"Yes. To all of the above." He raised one suggestive eye brow.

Most disarming.

She cleared her throat and said, "I'll call room service."

He reached for the morning's *Hong Kong Star*, which was lying on the bureau, and devoured it like Rip Van Winkle trying to catch up on what he missed in the world.

In a few minutes the bellboy arrived again. As he looked at the stranger, draped only in a bath towel, his expression grew even more dumbfounded than it had been earlier. C.J. gave him a generous tip.

The man folded up the paper and laid it aside. Taking a swallow of coffee and a long drag of a Marlboro, he sat back in his chair looking relaxed and content.

C.J. felt anything but content. Her nerves were frayed, and she stirred her coffee, round and round. She had imagined that the stranger would quickly bathe, nap and eat, then tell her about Alan and go on his way. It wasn't working out quite that way. She had to find a way to ask her hundred and one questions, and then get him out of there.

"Well, Sis," he said. She dropped her spoon, sending it clattering onto the table. She reached to grab it, but he put his hand on top of hers. She felt the strength in it. Stiffening, she looked at him in surprise. "My male ego would like to think it was my magnetism that attracted you and made you plead with me to come here as your kept boy, but I know better. What now?"

"We need to talk." She pulled her hand away.

"True. Shall I call you Sis, or Seejay—sounds like a Pakistani name."

"Pakistani? Oh, I see. My goodness, no. Straight mid-west. My name is C period, J period. Just initials."

Once again, she realized she had been so caught up with Alan's problems that she hadn't asked the man who he was. "What's your name?"

"C.J. isn't a name."

Had she heard him right? "It's mine." She tried again. "What's yours?"

"No one names little girl babies just letters. That's usually something they do to themselves to hide sickeningly sweet names like Bunnie, Queenie, Missy, Muffy—"

"Most little girls' names are not sickeningly anything. What's your name?"

He pursed his lips. "C.J. Hmm. Is it Carrie? What about Cecilia? Or Carla? Now, there's one worth initializing."

Her eyes narrowed with irritation. "No!"

"Carmen? Charmaine?"

"Knock it off!"

"Aha! You're not afraid to speak up! That means it must be a delicate, feminine name—one that's totally unsuitable, right?"

C.J. felt the color drain from her face at those words.

"How about Clarissa? Clarice? Cassandra?"

How can I stop this dreadful man? How can I get him out of my room, out of my life? To think I invited him here! I must have been crazy. "I have politely asked your name a number of times," she began. "The least you can do is answer. You are, after all, sharing my room, my food, my—"

"Yes?" he leaned closer.

She seethed.

"All right." He backed off with a grin. "The name's Kane. Darius Kane."

"Oh." She leaned back in her chair. The name meant nothing to her; she hadn't come across it in any of Alan's papers.

"Yes, well, that's the reaction I get from a lot of women."

"I didn't mean that I'm not interested."

"Oh?"

She fumed. "I mean, it's just that I was hoping that your name might mean something to me. But I've never heard of you before."

His eyes twinkled. "Let's go back to how interested you are."

She jumped up. "Look, Mister Kane—"

"Darius," he interjected, another grin playing on his lips. "No woman calls me Mister when my clothes are off."

"Mister Kane! My brother is missing. I'm at the end of my rope. No one will help me. I've been fighting here, literally fighting, with the police, immigration, the airport people. I just. . .I just. . ." She crossed the room and sat on the bed, arms folded, trying to calm herself.

"Hey, Clementina." Darius got up from the table and walked to her side, placed a hand on her shoulder, then bent toward her. "Forgive me. I should have realized. It was just a joke. A bad one. Forget it, okay?"

His apologetic words were her undoing; her eyes welled with tears. He was so close that she could smell the soapy cleanliness of his skin, feel the heat from his hands, and she turned her head away, more upset than before.

"I never cry, you know." She brushed a tear from her cheek. "I haven't cried since I was sixteen and the boy I was madly in love with showed up at a beach party with an eighteen-year-old. Now I've cried twice in as many hours. I don't know what's wrong with me."

"C.J., I'm sorry."

It sounded too much like pity. "Stop!" She stormed across the room to the dresser and leaned over it, seething. She had been taxed beyond endurance by the whole frustrating situation of not being able to find Alan, not to mention the reticence of the police, and now she had to deal with an unnerving reaction to Darius Kane. She couldn't stand it anymore; something had to give. She spun around and glared at him. "It was a mistake to involve you. You don't know a thing, do you? Nothing. I should have left you with the police. I should have let you rot in jail!"

Darius yawned and sauntered to the far side of the double bed. "Let me know when my clothes come back. In the meantime, I'm going to take that nap you mentioned."

With a single, fluid motion, he pulled back the covers, then lay down, stretching the length of the bed and then some. With a contented sigh he pulled the covers over himself and flipped the towel he had been wearing to the floor.

C.J. stood speechless as she watched the towel fall, appalled at his presumption in getting into her bed. She gave what she hoped was a withering look, but immediately saw that her glare had been wasted. His eyes were shut, and his chest moved with the calm rhythm of sleep.

How can he do that? she wondered, one hand on her hip. She was beside herself with anger, and he had the nerve to fall asleep as soon as his head hit the pillow. He had to be the most infuriating man she had ever met. She hadn't even asked him any of her questions, and there was so much she needed to know.

She had an urge to push him off the bed in such a way that his supercilious posterior would be rudely greeted by the floor.

She stepped closer to him. How could anyone who was so devilish when he was awake look so angelic when he slept? She was struck by the dark hollows beneath his eyes. He looked exhausted, vulnerable, and something more—as if under that easy grin and behind all the jokes there was sadness, a deep hurt. This was crazy, she thought. She had no business doing two-bit analysis on someone she hardly knew.

Darius Kane. She looked down at him and shook her head. "Dangerous" Kane would have been more suitable. He was a mystery to her, yet, for some reason, he had decided to trust her. She knew that only trust would let a man like him fall asleep in such a defenseless way. He seemed to be a man who lived on the edge of society, yet he'd put himself under her protection, for a little while, at least.

She wearily rubbed her forehead with her fingertips. Why am I angry with him, anyway? she wondered. Unable to answer her question, she switched off the lamp that was shining on his face, sat down on the nearby chair and watched him sleep as the night grew dark.

CHAPTER 4

C.J. was vaguely aware of sunlight flooding the room, and she rolled to her side, burying her face in the pillow. As she turned, she bumped something with her foot and gave it a good kick to get it out of the way.

"Ouch! What the—"

At the sound of a man's voice, her eyes opened wide. The events of the previous day came back with the chilling clarity of a scene in a horror movie. She sat bolt upright, not looking at him, and giving a prayer of thanks that she was fully dressed and on top of the covers.

"If you wanted to wake me up so badly, there are nicer ways to do it than with a kick," Darius said. She peeked over her shoulder at him, then quickly scrambled off the bed before she turned to face him again.

He was on his side facing her, his elbow propped up on the pillow, and his head resting against his hand, a look of bemusement on his face. His hair was tousled, a few stray golden locks falling over his forehead, and his eyes were still heavy from the long night's sleep. The flutter her heart gave at his appearance was more than a little disturbing.

"I was hoping you were just a nightmare," she said, madly trying to smooth her clothes and her hair.

His laugh was low, husky and intimate. "It was nice of you to join me."

Bristling, she folded her arms. "Before you get too smug about your irresistible charm, I suggest you try sleeping in that spindly little chair all night. It'll give you a good idea of what was *really* irresistible on this side of the room."

Surprise flickered across his face, and then he laughed.

"If that's how you feel," he said with a rueful look, "I'll go."

Slowly his foot emerged from under the covers, then the calf of his leg, up to the knee. Now fully awake, C.J. remembered his state of undress.

"Wait a minute," she cried, hurrying to the phone, not daring to face him. "I'll call for your clothes. I'm sure they're ready. In fact, they should have come back last night. Don't do anything rash."

"All right, dear sister, you can turn around again. I'll stay covered up in your bed as long as you like. I'm not complaining."

She rolled her eyes as she called the front desk. Peeking at him, she saw that the wayward foot was back under the covers, and she sighed with relief.

Before long a bellboy, a different one this time, appeared with Darius's clothes. He walked into the room, then looked from C.J.'s rumpled state to Darius in the bed. "Miss Perkins," he said, bowing slightly, then hung the clothes in the closet.

"Oh, my God!" C.J. was horrified at the bellboy's expression.

Darius chuckled, "I'm sure it's not the first time—"

"It's not funny!" She was still staring at the hotel door.

"Oh, what tangled webs we weave..."

She turned to glare at him, but when her eyes met his, the mirth he exuded hit her. Against her will, the sides of her mouth began to rise, and she knew that if she allowed herself to look at him one minute longer, she'd laugh out loud, and this was not a laughing matter. One's reputation was not to be trifled with.

My God, she thought, I'm thinking like Mildred! At that she did give an amused chuckle, then grabbed some clothes and went off to shower. For some reason, one she absolutely refused to contemplate, she found herself taking extra care with both her clothes and her makeup.

She emerged from the bathroom in an emerald green blouse, pearl gray slacks, and low black heels. Darius's eyes drifted over her appreciatively, causing a further rush of color to her cheeks.

He had dressed in jeans and a crisp plum colored shirt. She saw once again, as if she needed it, how handsome he was. Her conservative, almost matronly outfit felt dowdy in comparison.

His rolled-up sleeves revealed again the scars on his forearm, causing her to remember how little she knew about him. The day before, she hadn't allowed herself to think about the type of man who would be running around Southeast Asia with no passport or other identification. But this morning that was all she thought about. The possibility that he was some sort of criminal was all too real.

He had ordered a pot of coffee, *char siu bau,* and a newspaper as she showered.

By the time he finished his pork bun, two cups of coffee, and the morning paper, C.J.'s patience had vanished. "Who are you?" she demanded, her fingers tightening on her coffee cup. "What do you know about Alan?"

He slowly folded the newspaper. "I'm just an American who finds this part of the world suitable. As to your brother, I know very little, except that his name is mixed up with the White Dragon theft."

"Theft?"

"You didn't know?" He looked at her as if he couldn't believe her surprise.

"No, no one will tell me anything. What theft? What is the White Dragon?"

"You're kidding me. You've got to know something."

She stiffened. "I beg your pardon!"

"You came here by yourself?" he asked. "Into this mess with no idea what's actually going on?"

"Hard though it may be for you to believe, I came here because my brother is missing."

"But this is…" He stopped.

"This is what?" she demanded.

He studied her as if taking in the measure of her, not wanting to believe her, but realizing he did. "Dangerous. It's very dangerous." His voice was soft but serious.

She blanched. "Tell me everything."

He paused for a moment. "The white dragon is a small jade statue, no bigger than a large apricot, carved during the Chinese T'ang dynasty, around 750 A.D. The jade the artist used was white, not the usual green, and it was absolutely flawless. It was intricately carved into the shape of a dragon and presented as a gift to the Emperor of China."

She looked at him blankly. "I see. It sounds very valuable."

"Priceless."

"And now it's been stolen?"

"That's right. It belongs to the People's Republic of China. The Chinese agreed to send it along with some other T'ang sculptures on a tour to major European museums. The pieces got no farther than Hong Kong. They were stolen from the Museum of History. It's a very embarrassing situation for the Hong Kong government, and since this is a British colony, the British feel responsible. The Chinese are furious."

She shook her head in disbelief. "All those governments involved. How could it happen?"

"It took a pro. It was a slick, well-planned operation."

She thought about everything he told her. "When did this happen?"

"Over a month ago," Darius replied.

"A month!" Relief filled her. "Alan was in Malaysia a month ago. How could he have known anything about it?"

"You tell me. I've told you all I know, C.J. Your brother's name has been mentioned in and around Hong Kong in connection with the theft, but there's no proof that I know of that he stole it."

"Of course not, he's innocent."

"That's not what's being said," Darius told her.

She felt her throat constrict and bit her bottom lip. "He is! It's just…he's not…" She couldn't go on. The paper she'd found in Alan's room had Bai-loong, the Chinese words for White Dragon, written on it. She shut her eyes, concentrating on blocking the thought that wanted to be born. It was more than coincidence, but it didn't mean Alan was guilty.

Darius frowned, more at himself than at her. And then, with an expression that said he had no idea why he was allowing himself to get involved, he stood and held out his hand. "Come on. Let's get out of here."

"Where are we going?"

"Anything is better than going back to the Luchow police station, isn't it?"

Spurning his hand, she picked up her large, leather shoulder bag.

He didn't seem to believe Alan was innocent, and she needed to know why. If she went with him, perhaps she would find out.

They rode the elevator in silence and didn't say a word as they approached her car. The streets of Kowloon were bustling, as usual. Tourists from all over the world packed the area daily to look for bargains, merchants from throughout Asia were there to oblige them, and in the midst of it all thousands of resettled mainland Chinese lived, worked and played. At all hours of the day and night, Kowloon was one of the busiest places on the face of the earth.

"May I?" Darius asked as he took the car keys from her hand, unlocked the doors, then got into the driver's seat.

C.J. decided not to argue with him. Hong Kong's traffic filled her with terror. Not only were the streets horribly congested, but the cars drove on the left side of the road. It was the opposite of the U.S., and the same as in Britain. She was all right as long as she was driving straight ahead, but making a left or right turn was an adventure. More than once she had ended up facing oncoming traffic.

"Where are we going?" Since he hadn't offered to tell her, she decided to ask. It was her car, after all.

"To the American Consulate. Eventually." He swung into traffic.

"Oh, yes, you do have a fondness for it, I recall."

Her wry comment provoked a small smile from him. "Since the consulate is on Hong Kong Island, while we're there I want to pay a visit to an old friend, Jimmy Lee. He lives on the Peak."

Fine, she thought. Now we're going on social calls! What's next? Charity work? She folded her arms and said nothing.

A little while later C.J. realized that Darius Kane led a charmed life. He not only easily navigated the heavy traffic in the Cross Harbour Tunnel, the underwater passage that connected the city of Kowloon with Hong Kong Island, but even more astounding, he found a parking place right by the station where they could catch the Peak Tram.

"Do you mind taking the tram instead of driving?" he asked.

"No," she said, although she was surprised by his choice.

"I've always enjoy the ride. The view is terrific, and it's actually the fastest way to Jimmy's house since it goes straight up."

Despite her previous irritation, she couldn't help but smirk at the thought that "Dangerous" Kane liked train rides.

The green funicular railcar arrived, and they got in. As they climbed Victoria Peak, one of the most exclusive areas in all of Asia, they looked out over the harbor.

Darius draped his arm over the back of her seat, then bent closer to point out an ancient Chinese junk sailing by, its red, ribbed sails catching the wind and carrying it efficiently along. To her dismay, she felt more intrigued by Darius than the junk. And she didn't even care for the arrogant man!

As she watched, the hydrofoil that carried passengers from Hong Kong to Macao every half hour sped by, skimming over the water at a tremendous speed. The contrast between the two boats was as good an image of Hong Kong as C.J. would ever hope to see.

When the tram reached the uppermost station, they got off.

"It's a bit of a walk to Jimmy's, but there's no better way to see Hong Kong than from up here," he said. "It feels like you're on top of the world."

"It's beautiful. Absolutely beautiful." She looked out over the busy harbor sparkling in the bright sunlight. "This is the place to be when you don't have a care in the world."

"It's hard to believe that in a few years Britain's lease will run out and it'll be turned over to Communist China. It will change, but no one knows yet how much. All we know is what we have here now is a little piece in time, a bit of history that may be forever lost."

She stole a glance at Darius as he gazed out at the harbor, a solemn look of gloom and loss in his eyes. For all his easygoing charm, she still sensed a pervasive unhappiness about him. She wondered why, wondered what caused him to be in this place, living the way he did...being picked up by the British authorities.

But outwardly, what a picture he made with his strong profile, straight nose, and green eyes fringed by long, thick lashes. The golden highlights in his hair glistened like newly discovered gold whenever the bright sunlight peeked through the shade of the trees to find him. She would love to paint this scene of Darius and Hong Kong harbor from the Peak.

"There's Jimmy's place," he said after a five-minute walk. His expression changed to a smile as open and genuine as a twelve-year-old's.

Set well back from the street stood a large, white stucco house with high glass windows facing the harbor and a sharply angled roof.

A high white stone wall with a massive wrought-iron gate surrounded the home.

The butler obviously recognized Darius, and invited him and C.J. into the house. They were led through an elegant, marble-floored entry hall into the living room. The room was stark, yet breathtaking, dominated by a wall of windows providing a view of the island and the sea beyond. The walls were white. Chinese designed carpets covered the polished hardwood floors. Tall, leafy fig trees and lush green ferns graced the room, and Buddhist sculptures were the only artwork. The sofa and chairs were white.

C.J. chose a seat near the windows. In a short while the butler appeared with cooling gin fizzes for them both.

"Darius! You're back!" a slightly accented voice cried out.

"Jimmy!" The two warmly clasped each other.

C.J. studied the man who had just entered the room. Jimmy Lee appeared about Darius's age. He was tall, though not as tall as Darius. His features were as classically chiseled as a traditional Chinese painting, while his body was trim and muscular. The smile on his face made it obvious how he felt about his friend's visit.

They stepped back from each other. Jimmy's brow knitted slightly. "It's been too long, Darius," he said. "I was worried this time."

Darius laughed. "Can't count me out, Jimmy. You've got to learn that."

Jimmy didn't join Darius's laughter. "You're human. Don't forget it. Buddha might not like such arrogance."

Darius ignored Jimmy's warning, placed a hand on his friend's shoulder and turned him toward C.J. "I'd like you to meet Miss C.J. Perkins."

Jimmy bowed slightly.

Darius continued, "C.J., this is my best friend, Jimmy Lee."

"Pleased to meet you," she said, standing and extending her hand.

"And you," Jimmy replied as they shook hands. She felt that in the moment Jimmy had sized her up and filed her into a computer-like brain.

"C.J. is trying to find her brother, Alan," Darius explained. "He went to Luchow and hasn't been seen since. Now the police are asking about him and the White Dragon."

"Bai-loong...I see," Jimmy said thoughtfully. "Please sit down, Miss Perkins. I am sorry to hear your brother is missing."

Something about the way Darius spoke and the way Jimmy exuded control made her believe that if anyone could help her negotiate the mysteries of Hong Kong, it was Jimmy. She told him her brief story.

He nodded as she spoke, neither asking questions nor offering explanations. "I will make inquiries, Miss Perkins, and do what I can," he said when she finished. He held out his hand to her. "But for now, permit me to show you my garden. It is in the Chinese style, with small shrubbery, rocks and a pond, in many ways similar to what Westerners think of as a Japanese garden, and in many ways different."

"I would love to see it." C.J. took his hand and stood.

Jimmy tucked her arm in his and turned to Darius. "My friend, I would enjoy hearing some music from you. I know it's been a few weeks, so we'll leave you to practice."

Darius smiled. "I thought you'd never ask." He walked across the room to large French doors and opened them to a room with a grand piano at the far end. Gold upholstered chairs faced it. As Darius stepped into the room, Jimmy Lee escorted C.J. into the garden.

A feeling of peace and tranquility permeated the landscaping. Jimmy was telling her about the different plants when the sound of rich glissandi and complex chords drifted out to them in rapid succession.

"That's Darius?" she asked, incredulous.

"Yes. Outstanding, isn't he?"

She listened, and soon the opening practice notes ended, and he launched into a familiar piece.

"I know that work," she said, looking at Jimmy. "My God, it's Rachmaninoff's third piano concerto! I'm no musician, but I know it's quite difficult."

"Yes," Jimmy laughed. "I know, too."

"But he…" She listened for a while longer. "He plays beautifully!"

"You haven't known Darius long, have you?"

She shook her head. "We just met yesterday."

"Yesterday!" He sounded shocked.

"Yes. Why?"

"Nothing…nothing at all." He seemed to study her even more carefully than previously before he continued. "I've known him for many years, since I was a student at Harvard. I even spent a few summers living with his family in Boston. That's where I picked up this American accent."

C.J.'s eyebrows rose at that.

He grinned. "Well, at least my British friends here think I sound like a Yankee. But back to Darius…anyone who's around Darius for any amount of time soon learns of his love, his passion, for music. He's good. Great, in fact. He could have been one of the outstanding pianists of our time."

"Could have been?"

"There was an accident," Jimmy said, watching her reaction.

"Accident?" she questioned. "But he seems fine."

"You said you aren't a musician, which means that you, like myself, don't hear things, flaws, the way Darius does. What can I say?" He shrugged.

C.J. shook her head and followed Jimmy as he continued along the garden paths. The romantic music filled the small garden, capturing her in its web, the beautiful music and the man who performed it with such emotion and passion boring their way deep into her soul.

Darius practiced nonstop for over an hour—demonic dances of Liszt, relentless rhythms of Prokofiev, and mystic auras of Scriabin. While he played, C.J. and Jimmy drank gimlets on the veranda, a gentle breeze blowing onto the hill from the harbor. Jimmy told her about Hong Kong, his banking business, and every so often asked a question or two about Alan and Luchow. C.J. found Jimmy a charming conversationalist. He was witty, kind, and pleasant to be with. Still, more than half her attention was on Darius and his music.

Yesterday, when she'd met Darius, he had seemed like a wild man. If he had announced that he was the real Tarzan, she wouldn't have been surprised. But since then she had discovered him to be gentle and cultured, with talent that could have led to the world's top concert halls. Yet he lived in Asia without even a place to lay his head. It was puzzling.

As the sun rose higher and the humidity climbed, Jimmy decided it was time to go indoors.

"He would go on all day if we didn't stop him." Jimmy chuckled as they entered the music room. Darius was playing Chopin.

They listened until the piece ended, then applauded.

Darius looked up, startled to see them, as if the music had transported him to another time or another place, and it took a while to register where he was now.

Then he smiled, and C.J. felt her heart melt.

She and Jimmy walked toward the piano. Darius's eyes locked with hers as she approached, the luminous green of the wilds seeming incongruous to her in this elegant environment.

"You play beautifully," she said, surprised at the slight catch in her voice.

Darius glanced at his watch. "Look at the time! How could you let me play so long?" he asked.

C.J. and Jimmy looked at each other and laughed.

Darius turned to Jimmy. "We've got to get to the consulate, I'm afraid. I 'lost' my passport in Macao."

"Lost your passport? What happened?" Jimmy looked concerned. "Was it the counterfeiters?"

"They won this round, I'll admit. But I'll win the next. I was set up. Facing twenty-five years from the police—and that's the good news."

"So how did you get out?"

"Overland," Darius replied.

"Overland? That's impossible."

Darius grinned.

"Kane, no one waltzes through the People's Republic of China. I don't care how clever he thinks he is."

"What if he knows he's clever?"

Jimmy shook his head at Darius's answer, "Someday, Darius…"

"Don't worry, Jim. You know I always find the back door first. It's only a sucker who gives himself just one way out."

C.J. suddenly realized what they were talking about.

She felt her eyes widen in surprise as she looked at Darius. "You don't mean you were crossing into Hong Kong from the Communist border when the Luchow patrol picked you up?"

The two men glanced at each other.

"But that's impossible. The Chinese Army patrols…" she began, then stopped, realizing his story was absolutely true. She shook her head in amazement. "You did look as if you had just stepped out of the jungle."

"One visit to Sarawak and she sees headhunters under every leaf. I'm sorry to disillusion you, but there are no jungles along the Chinese border," Darius said.

"I don't care. You looked like it anyway. No wonder you were tired! It's astounding you're not dead!"

"Such compassion," Darius said to Jimmy, cocking his head in her direction. "Given a choice between the PRC and those boys in Macao, I made the right decision."

Darius and C.J. moved toward the door, Jimmy just behind them.

"Darius, why don't you two stay here until things die down."

Darius shook his head. "I don't think that'll work."

"At least get out of C.J.'s room. Use a different name and find a new one in the tourist area."

C.J. couldn't believe what she was hearing. All this time Jimmy had said nothing about her story, and now he was implying that he knew about it, and knew they weren't safe. Darius told her this quest of hers was dangerous. She was finally beginning to believe him.

"Probably so," Darius said.

"What will you do?" Jimmy asked with a frown.

"I'll watch her," he said, then hurried her out the door.

She wanted to ask why Jimmy had said what he did, but before she could say a word, Darius was walking rapidly along the sunny, shimmering hillside toward the tram. She gasped "Wait," a couple of times while halfway running to keep up with him, but he seemed completely lost in thought.

She was breathless by the time they reached the tram, but finally had a chance to step in front of him and ask her questions. "What did Jimmy mean? Why did he say my room wasn't safe? Who are you going to watch?"

He looked at her as if surprised by her words. "You, of course."

"Me? Why?"

"I'm sure it's just a suspicion on Jimmy's part. If he knew anything for sure, he'd tell us."

"But why the suspicion?" she asked. "You two practically talk in code!"

"Maybe he's worried because I'm with you," he said softly. "They might see me and think you know a lot more than you're pretending to."

"What?" she gasped, growing increasingly agitated with every answer he gave.

"They might think there was actually some purpose to your crazy actions," he added, then tapped the tip of her nose with a smirk.

"They? Who are *they*?"

"Who knows?" he confessed. "I suspect you never should have talked to me. And I shouldn't have been so ready to accept all that you offered. If I've added to your troubles, I'm sorry."

She was stunned by his words, not sure how to respond, when the tram's arrival prevented her from having to say anything. She and Darius were swept along in the group of people getting on.

At the foot of the Peak they hurried to C.J.'s car and sped off toward the consulate. In a short while, Darius said, "Stay calm. It seems we're being followed by a black Mercedes."

"You're joking," she said as she peered at the side view mirror at the cars following. "There are lots of black Mercedes in Hong Kong, I've noticed."

Darius turned left at the next corner. So did the Mercedes. He made another left after a few blocks, ditto the black car.

"Oh my God," C.J. gasped. "What are we going to do?"

"It's probably safer trying to lose them than to make a run for the consulate."

She gripped the door handle, her face determined, her mouth dry. "Whatever you say, Dangerous."

"Dangerous?"

She hadn't even realized she'd said it aloud. "The name suits you. Trust me."

The black car was now out in the open behind them. "They know we've spotted them. Hold on, Carmelita!" He stomped on the accelerator while pulling out of his lane and into the oncoming traffic.

C.J. cried out and clutched the dashboard.

Hong Kong traffic was, as usual, all but gridlocked. But Darius easily squeezed past a Toyota that had been ahead of him, then swung in front of it. C.J. didn't even have time for a sigh of relief before she felt herself thrown against the passenger door as he spun into a right turn from the far left lane. It made her dizzy just watching the cars go by on the "wrong" side of the street, but when Darius threw in hopelessly reckless driving, she was ready for hysterics.

A string of blaring horns and blazing tempers followed in their wake.

She sat white-knuckled, clinging to the dashboard. Every so often she peeked at Darius, convinced she would see him with one hand on the horn and the other over his eyes so that he couldn't see the close calls or the carnage around him.

They careened through the city, weaving wildly through the traffic, but the Mercedes was never far behind. She was giving serious contemplation to crawling onto the floor when he said, "I think we're okay."

C.J. pried her stiff fingers off the dash and twisted this way and that to look around. The black Mercedes was gone. "Thank God! Shall we try the consulate now?"

"Sounds good."

He turned onto Garden Road where the American Consulate stood, and immediately made a U-turn. She was flung back against the seat, the car leaping to life as Darius gunned the motor. "I saw it, too," she said. A black Mercedes had been parked just outside the consulate. Was it the same one? She had no idea, but agreed with Darius that it was best not to chance it.

"We'll go to the hotel," he said. "I'll help you pack up and find another place to stay. Use a different name and you should be safe."

She stared at him. "What about you? Will you also stay at the next hotel?" she asked.

He gave her a quick glance, and turned back to the road.

"No."

"Where, then? Why not stay where I am?"

"That might not be a good idea."

She nodded. How could she have forgotten? "Right, you have a life. I just sort of barged in and took over, didn't I? God, where's my head? You've got other things to do! Important things...like your counterfeiters in Macao."

"Listen, the safest thing for you to do is to go back to the U.S. Let the police do their job. Jimmy warned us. There's something big going on here. Bigger than either of us knows."

"That scares me, I'll admit it. But I'm not going home until I find out what has happened to my brother." As she spoke, she stared straight ahead, not wanting to look at him, not wanting to admit to herself how after less than twenty-four hours with him, the thought of leaving was difficult. But she always was a silly sort of person that way. "If Jimmy Lee learns anything, will you at least let me know?" Somehow she managed to keep her voice calm.

"C.J., you need to leave here, you really do." He touched her hand as he looked at her, and almost immediately realized that pleading for her safety wasn't going to work. "All right, if anything turns up, I'll contact you."

He pulled into a parking space near her hotel. They cross the lobby to the elevator in silence.

"We have to get out of here fast," Darius said as they got off at her floor.

She nodded, feeling strangely abandoned, even as she derided herself for those emotions. She could handle this quite nicely all by herself. Just as she had been doing before Dangerous Kane entered her life. Or, had she?

Darius held out his hand for the key to her room. She couldn't keep her eyes from lingering a little too long on his hand, tanned and rugged, yet with fingers so sensitive they had made some of the most beautiful music she had ever heard.

She shook her head, kept the key and stepped in front of him to the door. She squared her shoulders as she slid the key into the lock, determined to pack quickly, get out of here and be on her own again —away from this man and his disturbing presence.

But when she opened the door and stepped into the room, she gasped in shock.

"Oh no!" She cried as she stormed inside. She heard Darius cry out, "Wait!" But she was too busy looking at her belongings on the floor, at the overturned bureau drawers, and emptied closet.

From behind the door, a hard, viselike hand gripped her arm while a heavy blanket was thrown over her, cutting off all light and air. She gasped in shock as a thick arm circled her waist and lifted her as if she were a rag doll. Someone pushed the blanket hard against her face, muffling her scream of terror.

She fought wildly to be free. Her arms were pinned down, but she kicked as hard as she could.

Suddenly she was flung roughly aside, helpless to stop or protect herself, and came up against something solid.

Her mind went black as she fell in a heap to the floor.

CHAPTER 5

"C.J., are you all right?" Fresh air filled her lungs as Darius untangled the heavy blanket and lifted it away from her.

"Oh God!" She sputtered as she sat up. "What happened?"

"A couple of men grabbed you before they noticed me in the doorway. That's when they pushed past me and ran. Since one of them had a gun, I wasn't about to argue."

"A gun? Here? In my room?" She felt even more light-headed than when the blanket was over her.

Gently, he pushed her hair back from her face and ran his fingertips along her cheekbones and forehead, his face filled with concern. "Does it hurt anywhere?" His voice was hushed, full of worry.

"No, I'm okay." She tried to stand, but was so woozy that before she got very far he scooped her up in his arms. Shocked, she put her arms around his neck as he walked toward the bed.

"Put me down! I don't need to be carried! I'm too heavy!"

"Don't be silly," he said softly. He held her as if she were a child, then lowered her to the bed and sat by her side.

"I just had the wind knocked out of me, I guess." She tried to smile, but found she couldn't—her heart was pounding too wildly. Between her fright and being in Darius's arms, she didn't know which made it harder for her to breath.

"Dr. Kane says a little rest is called for."

"Shouldn't we get out of here right away?" Her eyes darted toward the door, as if she were expecting to see a bunch of maniacs burst through it any moment.

"You have time to calm down. They won't be back that soon."

"Did you recognize them?"

"They looked like a couple of standard issue thugs. Hong Kong, like any big city, is full of them."

"You think it was just a random burglary, then?" She hoped he would say it was.

"No, but don't worry about that for now. Just rest. You're very pale. It won't do your brother any good to have you ill."

At the mention of Alan, a wave of fear swept over her. If people were coming after her on the off chance she might lead them to him...

She turned her head away from Darius and shut her eyes tightly, raising one hand to cover them, as she willed the scared, sick feeling to pass.

He took the hand she had raised and held it between both of his. "C.J.," he said. "Is there anything, anything at all, about this situation that you haven't told me?"

"Of course not," she said, trying to free her hand, but he only held it more firmly. After a moment she added, "It's just that hearing Jimmy Lee's warning, then the car chase, and now those men, right here in my room, I can't help but think that something. . ." She paused, lifting worried gray eyes to his green ones. "What if something...terrible...happened to Alan? What if he's..."

"Hush, C.J. There's no indication of anything like that. He's fine, I'm sure. You'll find him." He continued to hold her hand and she found her fingers tightening on his as if they had a mind of their own.

She tried to believe his words, to drive the horrible thought from her mind, but the more she tried, the more persistently it clung. Alan, her big, strong, wonderful brother, might be in real trouble, hurt, even— *No!* She groaned.

Darius, trying to calm her, placed his hand against her cheek. His touch was like fire, and it was all she could do not to reach out for him. Instead, she sat up quickly, then turned and place her feet on the floor; firmly on the floor.

"I don't know what more I can do," she whispered.

"You've tried," he said. "But this place, this situation is too dangerous. You're just not the sort of person who should get mixed up with thugs and low-lifes. You're such an innocent."

She looked up at him. His gaze was soft and gentle, and far, far too kindly. Quickly, she stood and took a few steps away from him, folding her arms.

"I won't give up, Darius."

"That's what I was afraid of," he said with a smile in his voice. "I guess that means we'll have to find him."

She faced him again, unable to believe she had heard him correctly. "We?" she whispered, remembering his insistence about leaving her.

He stood as well and stepped closer. "Yes."

If only I understood you, she thought, trying to ignore the flutter in her breast. "Thank you," she whispered, thankful she didn't have face these dangers, this strange, foreign, frightful area alone. His nearness soothed her, filling her with unexpected warmth.

Alarmed at her increasingly strong reaction to this man, this *stranger*, she reminded herself, she began to hurry around the room picking up belongings strewn on the floor, doing whatever she could not to think about Darius Kane. It was safer that way. The ever-present, practical creature who lived in her head forced her away to keep moving, to not stop, to not let herself feel. She was a loner, would always be one, and had long ago accepted that about herself. To think otherwise, especially about a man like Darius Kane, would only cause her unhappiness.

He lifted her suitcase onto the bed so that she could begin to pack it, an odd expression on his face. She prayed he hadn't realized the turn her thoughts had taken. If he had, she was quite sure he would be appalled by any such romantic notions on her part.

She was simply "good old C.J.," the down-to-earth one everyone else went running to when they had difficulties, the one everyone leaned on, needed...used. She had to be tough when those around her were falling to pieces, practical when they were lacking caution. The role didn't put her in a position to be the object of many men's desire. Many? Hah...not any man's desire. Or, at least, not any man she would have given a second thought to. Combining no likely man, with no second thoughts, she found herself, at age 28, in a laughably inexperienced state.

Darius had called her innocent. If he only knew!

She concentrated hard on packing her bags, with Darius helping as best he could, and she trying but failing miserably to ignore him.

She fastened the locks on the suitcase, then looked up.

Darius sat on a chair and took out a cigarette. He lit it, leaned back, and watched the smoke spiral toward the ceiling.

"So tell me," he said finally, his arm on his knee, his wrist bent loosely as the cigarette dangled between his long fingers, "how does Miss C.J. Perkins spend her time when she's not chasing down thieves and missing relatives?"

Glad to get her mind off its dangerous path, she began putting and cosmetics and toiletries into a tote bag. "I paint," she said.

"Paint? You mean houses, or pictures?"

"Pictures."

"Really?" He sounded interested. "Have you had any shows?"

"No."

"Oh?" He hesitated. "Your work is all commissioned, then?"

She paused. "In a sense. Yes, you could say that."

"Must be a very rich patron. A man?"

Was he insinuating what it sounded like? If so, he was even more deluded about her than she had imagined. "Good God, no." She shoveled more into her bag, eager to be off.

"But you did say you make a living doing this?"

"It's rather difficult to explain." He said nothing, but she could see the curiosity in his eyes. She paused, took a deep breath, then said, "I paint scenery. Mainly natural, garden scenes. Little ponds, the flora and the fauna—you know?"

"Yes."

"They didn't sell. Not at all. Not a single one." He nodded. "So I put some people in the scene. Potential customers gave them a second look, at least. So then I tried couples—a man and a woman, obviously in love. I even sold a few."

He smiled slightly, took one more puff and then stubbed out his cigarette in an ashtray.

She faced him, her back straight. "Then one day I heard one fellow say to another while looking at one of my paintings, 'What are they doing?' The other guy fellow, and said, 'Nothing.' Then they walked away. That got me to thinking."

One eyebrow lifted. "Yes?"

She shrugged, and in a clipped, curt voice explained, "Now my couples 'do' something. Or, I should say, *suggest* that something's going to occur shortly. And the paintings sell. I do live in Los Angeles, after all."

"You mean they're…"

"Slightly erotic."

He grinned. She looked at him, studying him, not sure what he thought. "C.J.," he said, "that's wonderful!" Then he laughed.

She turned back to her packing. She'd been through this before, yet, even as she tried to ignore his laughter, she couldn't help but glance his way. His gaze caught hers, and in his eyes she saw he wasn't laughing *at* her, but at the way she explained her work. The incongruity of someone like her creating erotic art…that was worth a chuckle. Slowly, her lips upturned into a smile. "At least they put food on the table. They're sensual, but no more graphic than the cover of a paperback romance."

"Oh? That risqué?" he teased.

He crossed the room to stand beside her, his gaze searching her too-serious face. "I imagine they would sell. Somehow, I'm sure they're very good. And what's most important is that you're doing what you love. To do the thing that's important to you—that's what makes you feel good just to be alive."

"Maybe."

He remained silent. She finished packing, and zipped her tote shut. She could feel his eyes on her, studying her. She wasn't sure how to react. Finally she looked at him. "What is it?"

"You. I don't understand you, Clarissa. Not at all." Something in his gaze as he spoke made her uneasy.

"Me? I'm just a simple, middle American girl."

"Simple? You're a complete contradiction! A fascinating, warm, open contradiction, I'll admit."

"Oh, sure!" She saw herself as being as straightforward as the proverbial Mom and Apple Pie.

"You're a very proper, mid-western lady, with a bold-as brass exterior, and an interior that's soft, loving and shy. You yell at policemen, take home strangers off the street—"

"I never—"

"And"—his gaze caught hers and held—"I'm sure you aren't one to casually make love to a man you share a mutual attraction with, which is something that about ninety percent of the unengaged women in this town would do, by the way. Yet you paint and sell suggestive pictures."

Her face reddened. She decided not to touch his comment about making love and concentrate on her paintings. "They aren't suggestive."

"Oh? Explicit, then?" He grinned.

"Maybe we should call them…*warm*." The corners of her mouth turned upward. They both broke into laughter, then looked at each other in surprise as the laughter faded and the realization that something more had developed between them, something that went beyond pleasant understanding, something that went beyond words.

She decided to double check the room, to make sure she was leaving nothing behind…anything to brush off the unsettling feeling he caused her. "Anyway, now you know my deep dark secret."

"Why a secret?" he asked.

Good question, she thought. She walked to the window and concentrated on the view—windows and views were her usual place of escape when she didn't want to face questions, people, or situations right under her nose. She placed a hand on the frame. Looking out, she said, "At times…sometimes…I feel like a failure. I wanted to be a great artist. I really did. To walk through the Museum of Modern Art and see my own work, a picture I had created. But it takes talent. I worked hard, and, technically, I'm up there with the best of them. But some things just can't be learned, no matter how dedicated you are."

"Not everyone can be Picasso." His words were quiet, sincere.

"You, on the other hand," she gazed at him as she remembered the beauty, emotion and perfection of his music, "you have talent."

His features hardened. "But no technique."

Jimmy's words about an accident came back to her, about the "flaws" in his ability. "I'm no judge, Darius, but for me, your playing was magical." She rubbed her hands together. "Anyway, I've lived with my shortcomings for a long time, and I accept them. But still, I like being able to create, even if it is just 'suggestive' little oils."

He folded his own hands and looked at them for a long time, then raised his eyes to hers. He stood, their gazes holding.

She took a step towards him, then another.

A loud rap on the door made her jump. "Police! Open up!" The pounding began again.

C.J.'s eyes were wide as she turned to Darius.

He winked, walked to the window, crawled out, and a second later was gone.

"Open this door!"

Her breath caught as she looked from the door to the window. Running to the latter, she leaned out over the sill. There was no fire escape, only a frighteningly narrow ledge along the side of the building. And they were four stories up!

She studied the darkened courtyard below, her heart in her throat. Darius was nowhere to be seen, but he hadn't fallen...she hoped.

Her hands shaking, she headed towards the door just as it was opened by the hotel's manager.

Standing with him in the hallway were two strangers in gray flannel suits. "May I help you?" she asked. "Is there a problem?"

A tall man, middle-aged, with thinning sandy brown hair and blue eyes, stepped into the room flashing his ID.

"Gilles, British Intelligence. Leaving?" he asked, looking at her suitcase.

"Is that a crime?"

"It all depends. My concern is the man with you. Where is he?"

She swallowed hard. "Are you talking about my brother?"

"We know he's not your brother."

"Of course he is! Ask the Luchow police."

"Alan Perkins was arrested this morning in San Francisco. He's being investigated in connection with the White Dragon theft."

The whole room swayed. C.J. reached out, grabbing the edge of the door, not wanting to believe what she had just heard. "Alan is in San Francisco?" she whispered.

"That's right. We have a few questions to ask of you and the man posing as your brother."

She shook her head. "My brother is no thief."

"That's for us to decide."

The other gray-suited man opened doors to the bathroom and closet. "He's not here, sir."

Gilles' eyes narrowed as he faced C.J. "Where is he?"

"Who?" She had no idea what to do or say.

"We suspect the man who was with you is Darius Kane. He's wanted in Macao. We wish to speak with him."

"I've never heard of him," she replied, not meeting Gilles's eyes.

"Please get your coat. I find it necessary to ask you to accompany us to the police station."

C.J. couldn't believe any of this was happening. Was she being arrested like Alan? And why? Because of Alan, or because of Darius? She picked up her jacket and purse and walked, like someone in a trance, between the two men. They led her out of the hotel to a police car. The hotel manager stood aside, his gaze reflecting his bafflement.

At the Kowloon Central Police Station, C.J. was placed in a small room with two wooden chairs, a desk covered with papers, an overflowing ashtray, and the remnants of tea and Chinese almond cookies. The smell of ash mixed with cold tea and stale cookies was nauseating. She pushed the food to one end of the desk, and sat as far from it as possible. She waited there for what felt like hours. It's all a ploy, she thought. They want to scare me so I'll tell them everything.

She was afraid just might work.

Finally an older man entered. He was of medium height, thin, with white hair and kindly blue eyes. So they think they're going to charm this out of me, she thought, steeling her resolve to say nothing. Although, she admitted, charm was certainly better than the alternative.

Jaw set, she glared at the man. Her hands shook so badly that even clasping them together didn't help.

"Miss Perkins, my name is Robert Davis. I work for the British government. I'm sorry for this inconvenience."

"I'll leave and save your conscience."

He didn't reply, but instead sat on the chair behind the desk. "First, my dear, we must talk."

She hated people who called her "my dear" almost as much as those who called her by her first name.

He coughed slightly, then handed her a picture. "Do you know this man?" It was Darius.

"Why?"

"You do, then."

"I didn't say that." She returned the picture to him.

"Help us locate him."

"Why?"

"We need to ask him a few questions."

"I don't understand any of this," she said.

Davis rose from the chair and paced around the room.

Suddenly he perched on the edge of his desk and leaned toward her. Tossing Darius's picture on the desk, he jabbed at it with his finger as he spoke. "If this is the man who was with you, his name is Darius Kane. He is an international bounty hunter. Do you know what that means?"

She felt her eyes widen at the news, and shook her head.

"Well, you should be shocked. It means he is the sort of man a decent young woman should have nothing to do with. It means he goes about the world capturing people, art objects, anything, for the reward they'll bring him. He doesn't do it for humanitarian reasons, and he doesn't do it like the police, because it's a job he can be proud of. He does it for his own selfish profit. He'll do anything, Miss Perkins, anything for a dollar." Davis stopped, and she was uncomfortably aware of his scrutiny.

"This man, Miss Perkins," he said, standing again, and looking down at her, "this man will even get to know an attractive woman and use her, play with her emotions, as a ploy to track down her brother. Then he can turn the brother over to the police and collect the reward. Of course, this sort of man always leaves on the next plane out."

C.J. felt dizzy, her stomach churning, as his words hit. She folded her arms tightly. "Why tell me this? I don't know him."

"We need to know what Kane knows about the theft. If he has proof Alan Perkins is behind it, we want that proof immediately."

"No!"

He put his hands on the desk and leaned over her. "Miss Perkins, of course your brother stole the White Dragon. Why else would Kane be with you now?"

"He's not with me!" She choked on the words. Hot, angry tears threatened, but she held them back, furious at his deception of her, and embarrassed at her sappy, sickening response to him. What an idiot she was!

Robert Davis walked to the door and held it open for her. His voice was subdued, almost gentle. "You can leave now, Miss Perkins. Thank you for informing us of Mr. Kane's involvement."

She looked at him in shock, then grabbed her purse and ran from the office.

CHAPTER 6

C.J. couldn't appreciate the beauty of San Francisco as she gazed out the window of the plane circling the city, awaiting clearance to land. The water was blue below her, but the only color she could see was green: the lush green of Asia; the green of the tall ferns of Sarawak; the green of a pair of eyes....

Forget him, C.J., she commanded. *The man used you; he never believed in Alan's innocence. You were a pawn for him, an avenue to get to his real target—the reward for finding the White Dragon.*

Oh well, it was better than being thrown over for another woman. Her self-deprecating joke fell flat, not even the slightest hint of a smile played across her lips. She closed her eyes and rested her head against the window as the pilot droned on about mild temperatures and fair skies.

She took a bus from the airport to downtown San Francisco. At the bus terminal she got a map and tourist book to gain some idea of the section of the city where she should stay. Next she found a talkative cab driver, and he readily recommended hotels, restaurants, places to see and how best to get around town.

She chose a moderately priced hotel near the very expensive Fairmont. The first thing she did after checking in was to locate Alan and learn when she could visit him in jail. Next she made a collect call to Columbus, Ohio to let her parents know what was happening. At least she could tell them where their son was, although they were anything but thrilled by the news. C.J. assured them that it was all a misunderstanding, and that Alan would be free in no time.

She put the telephone down and eyed the bed. Although it looked inviting after hours of sitting on planes or in airports, she couldn't abandon her big brother, alone and probably frightened, for something so selfish as a nap, so she wearily showered, changed clothes, and headed for the city jail.

She waited in a small visitors' room while her brother was summoned. An eternity passed before the door on the other side of the glass partition opened, and he entered.

"Alan!" She placed a hand against the glass, waiting for him to come near. He looked much older than he had three years ago when she last saw him. His shoulders seemed rounder, his dark brown hair thinner, and he had lost weight. It made no sense to her that there, in jail, was the brother she had always looked up to, the one she had always been so proud of. What had done this to him?

"C.J.! I knew I could count on you!" He pressed one hand against the glass opposite hers, and then smiled. In that moment, all the years drifted away. He was her big brother, and she idolized him. Tears filled her eyes.

"I'll do anything I can to help you," she said.

"I know." He withdrew his hand as he sat down, then ran his fingers through his hair making it more tousled than it had been. "God, I thought I might rot here! I've got a lawyer who I guess is pretty good. He's trying to get me out, something about false arrest. They've got nothing to hold me on, you know. Nothing."

"What happened? What's this all about?"

"They want to send me back to Hong Kong. To extradite me." The lines on his face had deepened, his dark eyes were flat, and his whole body drooped.

"Alan, listen to me. No one will tell me anything about what's going on here. Start at the beginning, okay, so I can help you."

He looked at her, startled by her words. "They didn't tell you?"

"No, nothing."

"I see." He sat back in his chair. "It's a simple story. I don't know why it's all gotten so confused."

"Go on."

"It began in Sarawak." He stared at her, seeming to wonder whether she would believe him. She nodded and smiled with encouragement. "I often went down to the beach to read. I liked being by the ocean to relax when the day's work was done. One day I spotted a raft drifting towards me. I know it sounds incredible, like a fantasy of some kind, but it's true! The raft was bobbing in the surf, coming closer and closer to the beach.

"There was something on it. At first I couldn't tell what, but as it drifted closer, I saw it was a man. I swam out, grabbed the raft and pulled it to shore.

"The man was dying. He was a sailor, and all the others on his ship were already dead. I tried to help him. I tried to save his life, C.J. I really did. But soon I knew it wasn't possible." He paused as if remembering that day.

"Oh, Alan, how terrible for you," C.J. said.

"Yes, it was. He knew his life was over, but because I had tried to save him, he offered me a favor. He said he knew where to find the *Bai-loong*, the priceless White Dragon of the T'ang dynasty. I don't know much about Chinese art, C.J., but I'd heard of that piece and how valuable it is. When he told me it had been stolen, I could hardly believe it. All I wanted to do was find it and turn it over to the proper authorities. There's a nice reward for it, you know. Anyway, the trail he gave me led me here. But as soon as I stepped off the plane, I was arrested."

"But why?"

He shrugged. "It seems my simple questions around Hong Kong just trying to find the Dragon, made the British think I know more about it than I do. They even seem to suspect I have it!"

She said nothing; his story made no sense. Why was he asking people in Hong Kong about the White Dragon when he already knew where it was? Clearly, there was more to the story. But still, why was he arrested? "It sounds like a terrible misunderstanding!"

"Yes, it was." He was silent a moment, and then smiled. "God, C.J., I just thought of something! If you're willing to help, I know how you can free me."

"Anything! Just tell me."

"There's a man here, in the Chinatown section." Alan was excited now. "He'll help me; help us. I know he will!"

"What do you mean? Is he a lawyer? What about bailing you out of here?"

"There's no need to spend money we don't have on lawyers or

bail! Believe me. Contact the man in Chinatown. Write down his address." He spoke quickly.

"Okay." She began fishing around in her big purse. "Here's my notebook."

"It's 99 Duncombe, just up the block from Grant Avenue off Jackson Street. The man's name is Mr. Yeng. He's very influential. I know the British will listen to him when he tells them I had nothing to do with the theft."

She raised both eyebrows. "Why should he tell the British such a thing? What does he know about this?"

"He knows enough. Give him the name, 'Chan Li,' and then say that I'm in prison and must be set free. Repeat that. Chan Li."

She wrote it down. "Chan Li. That's easy enough. But who is this man? What does he do?"

Alan sighed. "It's better if you don't know. Mr. Yeng will know. That's all that matters."

"I'm on your side, Alan, but how can I help you if you keep me in the dark? None of this makes sense!"

"What do you mean, 'in the dark'?" He scowled. "I've told you everything. And I need you, C.J. I need you, just like old times. I used to be able to depend on you. Now, will you help me, or are you going to abandon me, too?"

"Of course I'll help you." She stood, waving the notepad in front of her. "I've got my instructions. I'll be back as soon as I can."

Alan smiled at her. "You're a good kid."

"You'll be out of here soon." She felt terrible at having to leave him there. "I promise."

Between the time change from Hong Kong to San Francisco and her anxiety over Alan, she was ready to drop. It was night, and the sky was dark. More than anything, she wanted to go back to her hotel room and get some sleep. But how could she when that would mean Alan would have to remain in prison even longer. Even one minute more than necessary was more than her conscience could stand. Her stomach growled. She last ate on the plane somewhere over the Pacific, hours ago.

Forget about yourself, she ordered, while listening to every bone in her body creak with fatigue. Night was falling. A chill wind blew off the bay, and the fog had already rolled in and was blanketing the city.

Feeling light-headed, she hailed a taxi, then leaned back against the cushions with a sigh.

"Where to?" the driver asked.

"Grant and Jackson. Chinatown."

Grant Avenue was lit up like a Christmas tree, the street alive with activity. The cab crept along, hardly able to move in the crush of pedestrians and other cars.

C.J. soon ran out of patience with the slow pace. She handed the driver some money and got out a couple of blocks short of her destination. She pulled her light jacket tight around her. The breeze had turned cold. From open upper story windows, radios blared the wailing sound of Cantonese opera, while at street level, sales people chased down tourists to hand them flyers hawking shops and restaurants for dinner. Almost everyone seemed to stroll in one direction while looking the opposite way. People knocked against C.J. so often she felt like a bumper car at an amusement park. It almost felt as if she were back in Hong Kong, except that Hong Kong was about ten times more crowded, and the buildings much taller. Also, Hong Kong was a whole lot warmer.

Finally she reached Jackson Street. Alan had told her that the street she wanted was "up" from Grant. When he'd said up, she realized now, he'd meant it literally. Jackson Street rose steeply from Grant toward the center of the city. In the opposite direction, it roller-coastered down to the bay.

She walked up the hill into the hovering fog. The makeup of the street changed quickly, almost eerily so. From the bright neon lights of stores and restaurants along Grant Avenue, the shops on this street were closed and darkened.

As she ascended Jackson, through the fog she was able to see a street sign with the name Duncombe in Roman letters, and Chinese characters below them. Something made her slow her pace. When she reached the corner of Duncombe and Jackson, she realized that her foreboding had been warranted. Duncombe was a desolate-looking alley.

She peered down the alley. It was so dark that she couldn't see the end of it.

For all she knew, the black hole of Calcutta could be waiting for her down there. The old expression "being Shanghaied" struck her. It was used about people snatched off the streets of San Francisco's

Barbary Coast during the mid-nineteenth century and made to work on ships traveling to the Far East. Could Mr. Yeng, a man of influence, actually live in there?

Groping in her purse, she again pulled out the address Alan had given her. 99 Duncombe.

She put it away again and held her purse against her chest as if for protection. Her mouth felt dry as she took the first, tentative steps into the alley. A fog-shrouded streetlamp cast her shadow far in front of her, until even the shadow disappeared in darkness. The walls of the alley were mostly brick and stone with steel, roll-up garage doors interspersed between them. Dumpsters blocked the narrow sidewalk as she walked down the center of the pavement. She remembered reading in history books about the tong wars that took place in San Francisco's Chinatown in the late nineteenth century, and how rival tongs, similar to today's gangs, would line up in the dead of night facing each other in alleys like this one. Instead of guns and knives, they used hatchets. As they stared at each other, eventually someone would move—perhaps no more than the flicker of an eyelid. At that, the tongs would lunge together, their hatchets wildly swinging, inflicting horrible damage to each other. The next day, the city would wake to find the dead and dying.

Taking a deep breath, telling herself the days of tong wars were long past, C.J. plunged into the dark alley, her heels echoing loudly as she walked. Although she looked back over her shoulder toward the main street for comfort from time to time, the fog filled the air until, as she went deeper, she could see nothing more than a dismal blur.

A chill crept up her back, and her steps faltered.

A doorway! That must be it, she thought, as she hurried towards an old brick building. It was three stories tall, with only a few windows.

She stared at the heavy, dark wooden door before her. Perhaps this was just a warehouse? A daytime address? There was only one way to find out. She reached her hand towards the doorbell, but pulled it back as uncertainty gripped her.

She was sure Alan wouldn't send her anyplace dangerous, but maybe he had been wrong about the address. She glanced up and down the alley again quickly. She should just ring the bell and find out. But what if Mr. Yeng actually did live here? What if he answered the door and invited her inside?

She swallowed hard. Ring the bell, C period, J period, Perkins. Show them you can't be cowed by a little darkness and some fog!

She was again reaching for the bell when she heard footsteps coming her way.

Ring the bell! her mind cried. *You've got to help Alan.* She flung her hand toward the buzzer just as a pair of strong arms went around her, knocking her away from the door and pushing her deeper into the alley. At the same instant a hand was clamped tightly over her mouth, preventing her from screaming.

The man holding her was tall and strong. She struggled to get away, but she couldn't. His whispered voice was telling her something, but she was too frightened to make sense out of it. She struggled furiously before his hushed words penetrated her fears. "Stop it, C.J. It's me. Stop it."

She turned her head just enough to confront her attacker. As her eyebrows shot up in recognition, he took his hand away from her mouth.

"Darius!" she cried, putting her hand on her chest to still the mad beating of her heart. Her legs were ready to collapse from the fright he'd given her at the same time as she was overjoyed to see him here. The resulting confusion made her mad. "What the hell do you think you're doing, scaring me like that!" She waved her arms for emphasis.

"Not so loud." He spoke in angry, hushed tones. "What the hell do you think you're doing going up to the door of one of the most dangerous men in Chinatown?"

"What? But..." she sputtered.

"Come on!" Darius put his arm around her waist and hurried her out of the alley.

"No! Let go of me!" She struggled to free herself. "I will not go anywhere with you! What are you doing here, anyway?"

A slight metallic sound stopped her complaints. She clutched Darius' jacket and strained to see in the foggy darkness. A small tin can rolled toward them from deep inside the alley. They watched it in surprise, and then Darius pushing her back into a dark alcove formed by a garage door as a figure, short and slight, stepped from the shadows and ran past them to the street.

C.J. was afraid that her heart would stop from the scare Darius had given her, the effect of having him so close once again, and now this. She didn't know whether to be frightened or furious.

Still, she couldn't stop her fingers from tightening on his jacket.

"Who was that?" she whispered.

Without answering, he held her to his side as he quickly led her out of the alley. This time, she made no protest.

He hailed a taxi on Grant Avenue. "Mark Hopkins," he told the driver as they climbed in.

Even in her bewildered state, the name of one of the most elegant hotels in San Francisco came through with crystalline clarity.

She glanced at him in surprise. He had gotten a haircut since she saw him last, a casual razor cut, combed to the side and back. All in all, it suited him well. Too well.

Her eyes dropped to the jacket he was wearing. It was made of fine, soft leather, obviously expensive. What was going on here?

"The Mark Hopkins?" she asked finally. "Why are we going there?"

"I've got a room." He gave her a wink.

"A room? Hey, isn't that my old line?" She couldn't help a sheepish grin.

Yes, her old line.... Memories of the past few days came rushing at her. To her, Hong Kong would always mean only one thing: Darius Kane. She could remember perfectly the first time she'd seen him. How she had found the nerve to talk to him, let alone invite him to her room, she would never know. Then she remembered Darius in her hotel room, and the way he had teased her! And on Victoria Peak, overlooking the harbor, with the hot sun shining on his face and the bright azure sky as the backdrop. And Darius playing the piano...

Suddenly the words of the British inspector warning her against him drummed in her ears.

When she had been hurt and frightened by the burglars, Darius had comforted her. Yet the inspector had told her not to trust him. How well she remembered Darius' arms supporting her, his smile, that boyish grin that could make her heart melt or drive her to fury, his captivating eyes. But always, always, she thought of the inspector's warning, that Darius would do anything for money, including spending time with the sister of a thief.

She sat upright. "Take me to my hotel. The Golden Gate."

"What's the matter?"

"Leave me alone!" she shouted. "Let me out of here!"

The driver started to slow down.

"No." Darius leaned forward in the seat to speak to the driver.

"She's just upset. The Mark, please." He turned back to C.J. and took her hands. "Tell me what's wrong."

"What's wrong? Everything!" She freed her hands and clenched them as she spoke. "Why did you stop me from seeing Mr. Yeng? That man would have helped Alan. But you don't want that, do you? I don't want to see you. Not ever!"

She leaned forward toward the driver. "Stop this cab!"

The driver glanced back in his mirror and started to slow down again.

"She's my wife. Ignore her," Darius said to the man.

The driver nodded and sped up.

"What!" she cried, looking at Darius in horror.

"C.J., listen to me." He placed his hands on her shoulders and turned her to face him.

"No." She tried to push him away.

"Why?" he whispered, his grip tightening. "What's wrong? What have I done? Tell me, please."

His voice was soft, his eyes pleading. Such a good actor, she thought, a real pro. She glared at him. "I don't want anything to do with you. Is that clear enough?" But her voice was soft when it should have been harsh, weak when it should have been strong.

"Don't you?" he asked quietly.

She shook her head and looked away, her hands still against his chest.

"Then look at me."

She wanted to say something, anything, to prove to him how she felt, but no words came. Instead, she raised her eyes to his. As soon as she did, she realized her mistake.

Had she really forgotten how intensely he could look at her, and how his look could penetrate to her very core?

No longer did she hear the taxi's engine, feel the movement of the car; the only world that existed for her was Darius.

The cab pulled into the driveway of the Mark Hopkins, and the driver sat calmly, engine running, waiting for them to pay their fare.

As Darius paid, C.J. got out of the cab and waited until he joined her. "We need to talk, Darius," she said with conviction.

An eyebrow rose, but instead of answering, he led her across the elegant lobby to the elevator and up to the fourteenth floor. He opened the door and switched on the lights.

She walked halfway across the large room then stopped. She needed to face him, to talk, but the intimacy of the room and her memory of the way he had been there to stop her from walking—if she could believe him—into danger, made her heart thrum. She quickly continued on to the windows and forced herself to concentrate on the view.

San Francisco was breathtaking, its array of lights diffused and softened by the fog and mist. She felt as if she were high in the sky, in a strange never-never land with Darius.

"May I take your jacket?" he asked.

She faced him as his words broke into her reverie. "I'm only staying a minute. But I have so many questions…"

"Fine. I'll fix us drinks. Make yourself comfortable." He held out his hand until she gave up the jacket, then hung it up and mixed them each a brandy and soda.

She sipped her drink, the strong brandy warm and soothing, as she checked out his room. It was, in fact, a suite. Besides the bedroom, there were also a small sitting room, a dressing room and, of course, the bath. Some of the furniture appeared to be genuinely antique. A room like this must cost a fortune, she thought, as she settled into a tapestry-upholstered wing chair. She gazed at Darius, trying to figure him out.

"Did you rob a bank since I saw you last?" she asked.

"You never asked me about my finances, you know, before you lured me off to your hotel room. Maybe if I tell you now that I have money you won't be so eager to send me out of your sight."

"Don't bank on it." Her mouth twisted into a frown.

"You're right. You're not that kind of woman. I don't think you'd ever use someone like that. Not even if you needed to." He sat on an easy chair across from her, holding his glass with casual grace. "What can I do to interest you?"

"Tell me about Mr. Yeng."

"I was afraid you'd say something like that."

"Actually," she said, "I've changed my mind."

"Good." He grinned, and she felt her reaction to his smile in the fluttering in her breast. It took ail her concentration to remain businesslike. She drank more before she said, "What I want to know first is what you're doing here. Why are you in San Francisco?"

He swirled his drink around, then put it on the end table and leaned back in the chair as he studied her. "Would you believe me if I told you I know a sweet kid—no, not a kid, a woman—a warm, affectionate, beautiful woman, who's in way over her head and doesn't even know it? She's got a brother who's a real jerk—"

"Now wait—"

"He's an amateur playing against the pros." He leaned forward. "There's only one ending in this for him, unless he's really lucky. And I don't want to see the same thing happen to her."

Her jaw tightened. "If you told me that was your reason for being here, no, I would not believe you!"

His eyes flamed as his anger grew to match hers. He stepped up to her and placed one hand on each arm of her chair, then leaned down to face her. "I will assume that your brother is so addled over his thoughts of riches that he doesn't even realize what he's doing. If I thought he knew the kind of man Yeng is and still sent you there, don't think a mere jail would stop me from tearing him limb from limb."

She pressed herself against the back of her chair, trying to stay as far from him as possible. She refused to listen to his words. He was only trying to sweet-talk her; to use her. "Sure you would!" She spat out the words. "You have a lot of nerve trying to make me think your overwhelming concern for me brought you here! For one thing, you don't even know me! But I know you, Mr. Darius Kane. I know all about you. I know what you do for a living—if you can call it that! The British police told me. I know why you got out of that Hong Kong hotel room so fast. A bounty hunter! That's why you're here. It's not for me! The only thing I am to you is a link to Alan. And Alan, you think, gives you a link to the White Dragon. Well, you're wrong!"

He stood upright, letting go of her chair. "The British told you all that nonsense?"

"Nonsense? You told me yourself about the counterfeiters in Macao. Now it all makes sense!"

He stepped back from her, his expression strangely vulnerable. "C.J. . . ."

"What!" She stood up, too.

He gave a slight shake of the head. "Nothing."

"Nothing?" Arms folded, her eyes narrowed slightly.

He turned his back to her. "You're obviously exhausted. You probably didn't sleep on the plane, and when you got to the city, I suspect you immediately ran off to see that fool brother of yours. Now you have jet lag and you're hysterical."

Furious, she marched around him and looked him straight in the eye. "Hysterical? I am never, do you hear, never hysterical! I want to know what's going on! Who are you? What is your interest in all this?"

Hands in his pockets, he paced the room, then returned to his chair and sat, his eyes dark and thoughtful. "I know how it must sound," he said calmly.

She sank into the large chair again, her emotions topsy-turvy. She finished her drink as the silence spread between them, the minutes slowly, languorously ticking by. She didn't know whether she should believe anything he said; she knew only that she wanted to. She leaned back against the headrest as the liquor numbed her exhausted body. The longer she sat, the more that the fatigue she had fought against all day gripped her, the heavier her eyes felt.

"How did you find me?" she finally asked, her voice groggy even as she struggled to remain alert.

"Yeng's reputation and his lust for Chinese artifacts are well-known in Hong Kong—at least in Jimmy Lee's circle. Nothing happens in or around the Orient without that group knowing it, so, when I missed you at the jail, I decided to see if Alan would send you to Yeng's. Obviously he did."

Her eyelids kept shutting as Darius spoke, and she could barely hold her head up any longer. "No," she murmured. "Alan wouldn't..."

Darius placed a blanket over her lap and legs and lifted the glass from her fingertips. "Don't worry about it now, Carolina. Just rest."

She felt suddenly warm and cared for, as if a burden she had been carrying alone was now being shared. "Can't rest," she whispered. "There's no time..."

Then she sank into sleep.

CHAPTER 7

C.J. rolled over onto her back and stretched her arms before opening her eyes. The long night's sleep had been so welcome, so—*Oh, my God!*

She was in bed. She quickly tossed aside the blanket and stood. Shoes off, clothes on.

"Darius?" she called.

No answer.

Walking to the bathroom door, she called again, but received the same lack of response. The sitting and dressing rooms were also empty. Then she saw a piece of paper propped up on the night stand. She picked it up.

Dear Cleopatra Jasmine,

Sleep well, love, and don't worry. Wait for me here— you'll be safe. Trust me.

Darius

Wait for him? Trust him? If only she could! But with Alan needing her help, it was impossible for her not to go to her brother as soon as she could. She was halfway across the room when a word from the note sprang to mind, stopping her. "Love," he had written.

She shook off the thought, deciding it was probably just a Britishism he had learned in Hong Kong. But her gaze turned back toward the piece of paper. It would be so easy just to wait there and let Darius do the planning and the worrying for a while. But that would mean she had to trust him, and, logically, she couldn't. And one thing about C.J. Perkins: she was always logical. Painfully logical.

She quickly got ready to leave his room. At the door, though, she hesitated, then ran back to the night stand to pick up the note. She folded it carefully, put it in a zippered compartment in her purse so it wouldn't get crumpled, and then hurried out the door.

Back in her own hotel room, she discovered that a shower and breakfast could do wonders for one's well-being, even though she also realized, halfway through her omelet, that she never had gotten Darius to explain why he thought Yeng was a danger, or about the other man in the alley.

Bah! she cried silently. Why should she care what Darius Kane thought? He was there for one reason only—the White Dragon. Time to go see Alan. She put on a white blouse and peach skirt. Balancing on heels higher than she usually wore, she grabbed her huge bag and set out for the jail.

It took over an hour for officials to decide that she be allowed to speak to her brother again. When she entered the visiting area, he was already there.

"How did it go?" he asked first thing.

She sat down. "Are they treating you all right here?"

"Yes, yes. Now tell me about Yeng. What did he say? What was his reaction?" He looked ready to burst with expectation.

This was going to be harder than she had anticipated. "I'm afraid I didn't get to see him."

His face fell. "You didn't? Why not? Who did you see?"

"I, um, didn't see anyone yet."

"Oh." He frowned. "Too tired after your trip, I guess."

"No. I went there, but… Alan, tell me about Mr. Yeng. I've heard things."

"What do you mean, you went there, 'but'? But what? What have you heard about Yeng? Who have you been talking to?" He was angry, shouting at her.

"Calm down, Alan." She glanced nervously toward the guard, but he made no move. "I'll tell you all about it. I met a man in Hong Kong named Darius Kane who knows something about what's going on, and about the theft. I asked him to help me. I didn't know what to do, Alan, not even where to begin to find you."

"Wait a minute. You were in Hong Kong?"

"Of course. How else do you think I found you?"

"I sent a telegram to your apartment in Los Angeles!"

"Mom and Dad got a message from Sarawak that you had disappeared. I went to Sarawak then Hong Kong. British Intelligence told me you were here."

"I see…" He let all that sink in before he spoke again. "Okay, so you met this guy in Hong Kong. What does that have to do with Yeng?"

"Darius Kane is here. He stopped me from going to Yeng's. He said Yeng is a dangerous criminal." She searched Alan's eyes for a reaction, but the only one she saw was irritation.

His jaw set, and his tone became sneering. "How well do you know this guy?"

"Not well."

"Then why, in God's name, do you believe him? He's some stranger, and I'm your own brother! What's he doing following you from Hong Kong? It's not a cheap little jaunt, you know. It's not Oakland to San Francisco, or New York to Philly. How can you trust him? You shouldn't! He's after something, believe me. Maybe he wants me to stay here. Maybe that's why he told you tales about Yeng."

Alan's words reflected her own tormented thoughts perfectly. Why did she trust Darius Kane? Hadn't the British warned her? And now, Alan. She had always trusted Alan. Always.

But because of some stranger, she hadn't followed Alan's wishes. She was disgusted with herself. "Alan, who is Yeng? No one will tell me!"

Alan sat back in the chair and took several deep breaths before speaking in a much calmer voice. "Yeng is a very powerful businessman who knows many influential people. It's in his interest to keep relations between Hong Kong and Communist China peaceful, and that'll be even more important when the day comes that the Chinese take over Hong Kong…if it ever really happens. Anyway, Chan Li is a good friend of his, and through Chan Li he can learn that I am innocent. Mr. Yeng is powerful enough to see to my release." His speech finished, he folded his arms.

Suspicion grew in her at this blithe, too simple explanation. But there was no reason for Alan to lie to her, was there? "So that's all there is to it?"

"Of course! What did you expect? Underworld intrigue? Really, C.J., you sound as if you doubt my innocence, too! My own sister!"

Guilt gnawed at her, guilt over the truth of his words. "I'm sorry, Alan. Please forgive me. I won't ever doubt you again." Her gaze even, she continued. "It's that man, that awful Darius Kane. I'll never listen to him again, Alan, I promise." She stood to leave.

"That's great, C.J. I love you."

"I love you, too, Alan."

She hurried out of the jail, ashamed that Alan was still in prison because of her. Somehow, she would make it up to him.

She walked to the curb and was looking for a taxi when two Chinese men approached her. They were middle-aged, short, a little stout, and were dressed in dark blue business suits. They bowed.

"Miss Perkins?" one asked.

"Yes."

"We understand you wish to meet Mr. Yeng. He would also like to speak with you."

She looked from one man to the other in astonishment.

Their mouths were smiling, but their eyes were veiled. *I should feel happy about this,* she told herself. *Yeng sent someone to find me, which must mean he's interested in helping Alan. So why does my stomach feel as if it's got a lead weight in it, while my knees are turning into instant pudding?*

"Do not be afraid," the other man said. "We can understand your surprise at seeing us, but, be assured, we come as friends. We offer you a ride, unless you prefer to go to Mr. Yeng's residence on your own."

"I'm sorry. Please don't think I'm ungrateful. It's just that I'm surprised by this."

"Of course." They smiled and bowed their heads in tandem, reminding her of Tweedledum and Tweedledee.

"I'll come with you," she said, suddenly decisive. After all, Alan trusted Mr. Yeng, and she trusted Alan.

They thanked her and led her to their car. Won't Alan be pleased, she thought as she rode along, when he learns that Mr. Yeng wants to help him? She repeated the thought over and over like a mantra.

In no time, the car turned into Duncombe Alley. As they stepped out of it, someone opened the front door of Yeng's building.

With Tweedledum on one side and Tweedledee on the other, C.J. entered what she thought would be an old warehouse but instead was an enormous home. From the front door she stepped into a long hallway. To her right, the living room was elaborately decorated with Chinese-style rosewood and black lacquer furniture, and a riot of vermillion and gold artifacts, chests and lamps. It made her head spin just to look at it.

"This way please," a petite Oriental woman said to her.

The two men who had brought her there were no longer with her.

After the living room there was a more sedate but still impressive dining room; then, at the end of the hallway, she saw a long straight staircase with a door at the top of it.

After climbing the steps, the woman opened the door and beckoned C.J. to follow.

She entered an office. An enormous wooden desk took up most of the floor space. Behind it stood a small Oriental man, nattily dressed and wearing glasses.

"Greetings. I am Mr. Yeng," he said, bowing slightly.

And Darius had said she should be afraid of him! She could kill him with a flyswatter.

"So nice to meet you," she replied, shaking the hand he offered, then sitting on a yellow chair in response to his gesture.

"I understand your brother is being most unfortunately detained by the police in connection with the theft of the White Dragon." He sat, his folded hands resting on the desk.

"Yes, but he's completely innocent."

"I am sure that is so. Do you know why the police believe otherwise?"

"No, but whatever their reason is," she hurried to add, "Alan said you would know he's innocent."

"I?" A flicker of surprise showed in the man's otherwise impassive eyes.

"Yes. You have a friend who can prove it. Chan Li."

Yeng's eyes narrowed. "My...friend?"

"That's what my brother said. You will help him get out of jail, won't you, Mr. Yeng?"

"Of course. There's nothing for you to worry about. I'll take care of everything."

Relief filled her. Alan was right! She smiled broadly. "Thank you! You and Chan Li! I'll never forget either one of you. Never. I can hardly wait to tell Alan."

Yeng pushed a button beside his telephone, and in a moment the door to his office opened. A huge man walked into the room.

"My guest is through here, now," Yeng said, then nodded.

He must be my escort, C.J. thought as she rose from her chair, still smiling. "Alan and I will never forget your kindness," she added.

"Think nothing of it," Yeng said.

The large man stepped toward her. A white handkerchief in his hand flashed before her eyes as he lifted it to her face.

"What—" she began.

The handkerchief covered her nose and mouth, nearly smothering her. She flung her arms out, trying to push the man away, but she might as well have been trying to stop a truck. She needed air, fresh air, but she couldn't breathe, couldn't even scream. She tried to pull his hand from her face, but he seemed impervious to pain. A terror worse than anything she had ever known filled her as the room began to spin, then turn varied shades of purple. He bent closer to her, until she thought she was looking into the eyes of death.

Then everything went black.

CHAPTER 8

*S*he opened her eyes and saw nothing but blackness. She squeezed them shut again, her heart pounding, too frightened to move, to speak, to scream. She was on the ground, a cold, hard, rough surface…it felt like cement. The sense that a long, long time had passed, that she had been asleep for hours, filled her.

When she felt a little calmer, she opened her eyes again. Everything, still, was pitch black. My God, she thought, why can't I see? She sat up, reaching out in the dark to see if anything was near, but felt nothing. She blinked several more times, willing herself to see, but it did no good. Her breathing was rapid, and cold sweat beaded on her skin. What happened to her? What had that man done?

Not until she turned all the way around did she notice a small, faint bit of light, and nearly wept with, relief. Her sight was fine; it was the room that was black. The light was at floor level. It must be a door, she thought, with light from outside shining underneath.

On hands and knees, she crawled toward the light.

When she reached it, she felt around above the light and discovered that it was indeed a door. A way out. She stood, grabbed hold of the doorknob, turned it and pulled. The door wouldn't budge.

She pushed and pulled, trying to shake the door off its hinges.

"Help!" she cried, pounding on the wood. "Let me out of here. Please! There must be some mistake. I'm a friend. I'm not here to harm anyone."

Again, she tugged on the doorknob and pounded the door. "Please!" Her voice cracked with tears and fright. "Please, somebody! Help me!"

Hot tears fell down her face as she kicked at the door, hit it, then threw herself against it. What was this about? She shook her head, unwilling to acknowledge the obvious answer, fighting to calm herself so she could think.

But all she could think was that Darius had been right. Not Alan. Tears filled her eyes.

She slid her hands over the rough wall next to the door, hoping to find a light switch. She found one, flipped it up. To her amazement, the light came on.

Her gaze swept over the room. It appeared to be a small cellar with shelf-lined walls, the shelves packed with everything from auto parts and tools to old books. At least she could read to pass the time!

There were no windows.

The door had no keyhole, which had to mean it was padlocked or bolted from the outside, in the way of most cellar doors.

What now? Her eyes leaped to the door hinges.

She checked out the tools on the shelves. As she did, her eye caught the spines of the books. It figures, she thought. They were all in Chinese.

She rummaged through the tool boxes until she found a thin file. All she needed to do now was to pop the pins out of the hinges and she'd be free. She joyfully reflected on the idiocy of her captors to lock her in a room with a tool box.

The bottom hinge would be the first to go. She held the file against the top lip of the pin and pried. Even after several attempts it wouldn't budge. Looking closely at it, she saw that the hinge had not only gotten rusty with age, but was slightly bent.

She returned to the tool box for a chisel, a hammer and pliers, and soon was back at work. Every so often she would pound on the door for good measure, but her cries only echoed back at her.

The pins were stubborn. When she finally got one to move about a quarter of an inch she thought she should cheer.

It seemed that hours passed. No one came for her. Not only did her stomach feel empty, but thirst began to really bother her. Her arms ached, and blisters were beginning to form on her hands. Maybe her captors weren't such idiots after all.

One pin was about halfway out.

She threw down the pliers in frustration and sat on the ground, her back to the door. Tears streamed down her face.

I shouldn't let myself cry, she thought, I'll dehydrate faster. She envisioned someone opening the door in about forty years and finding a dried out corpse clutching a chisel.

She had no real sense of how much time went by before the bottom pin finally sprang free.

C.J. picked it up off the floor and kissed it. Then she looked at the other one. The top hinge meant no more sitting on the floor. She'd be stretching, trying to work with her arms above her head. The mere thought was painful.

She was so tired, sore and hungry that nothing really mattered at the moment but to rest. The blisters on her hands had broken already, causing blood to ooze from the torn skin. She tried not to think about how much they hurt.

She stood slowly, her body stiff and creaking from sitting on the cold cement ground. Her hands had already begun to swell and throb. She wasn't hungry anymore, but she was thirsty; her mouth felt like sand paper. She tried to lick her dry lips, but that provided no relief.

Yeng had done this. How could Alan have sent her here? He couldn't have known what kind of a man Yeng was. But Darius knew, so why didn't Alan?

"Darius," she whispered. "Darius, find me. Please."

She turned onto her side and curled up, miserable, but knowing that lying there and doing nothing was foolish. She walked around to loosen up, her muscles complaining with every step. Time to start on the second hinge. She picked up the chisel and hammer, but her hands ached so badly that when she tried to clasp the tools her eyes teared from the pain. She removed her half-slip and, using the file like a knife, tore it into strips. She wrapped those around her hands so she could hold the tools, then began to work again.

This pin was as stubborn as the first, and her progress was even slower, because of her awkward angle. She was beyond caring how she felt, but worked on and on, unwilling to give up and await her destiny without a fight.

"C.J.?" A slight tap on the door and the soft sound of a familiar voice caused her to freeze. Was it real, or a hallucination?

The whispered question came again. "C.J.?"

"Yes! Yes! Darius, I'm here." She threw herself against the door.

"Okay." She heard the rattle of a key, and in a minute the door was open and she was in his arms.

She held him tightly, burying her face against his neck. "I knew you'd come. I knew it."

He rubbed his cheek against her hair. "It's good to see you, kid," he said, his voice a little husky. "We have to get out of here. Be very quiet."

She stepped back from him and nodded.

He reached for her hand, then saw her makeshift bandages. With eyes full of concern as he looked at her, he asked, "What's happened?"

"Look," she told him, nodding in the direction of the hinges.

He said nothing for a moment, then looked at her with admiration. "Seems you didn't need me after all."

"I certainly did!" she said.

He led her to a staircase. They needed to get out of the basement, to go up to the ground floor. Once there, the area appeared to be clear. He had managed to get in through a small window in the back porch, but leaving that way would have involved a jump that he doubted C.J. could handle. He was going to try to get her out the front door. They headed down the hallway walking as quietly as they could.

At the sound of a footstep, Darius whisked C.J. into the dining room, hoping whoever was near would pass them by. The room was unlit, but the light from the hall and kitchen were bright enough that everything was visible. He hurried to the window to see if it offered any escape. They were about eight or nine feet up from the sidewalk. He could hold her until she was close enough to drop the rest of the way without breaking or spraining anything.

He pushed open the window when two men rushed him. "Run, C.J.!" he ordered, then stepped back to meet them.

All she saw was a mad tangle of arms and legs as the two men jumped Darius. She couldn't just leave him there.

She spotted a large Chinese gong at the entrance to the dining room, its wooden mallet on a stand beside it. She edged along the wall, keeping out of the men's reach, then picked up the mallet. It was surprisingly heavy. She lifted it high in the air as she stepped back into a shadowy corner.

The three men kicked and punched at each other, and she

watched them, awaiting her chance. Then, as Darius fought one man, the second one stood straight, reached into his pocket and pulled out a knife. With a flick, an enormous blade appeared.

Without hesitation, C.J. stepped behind him and swung the mallet down toward his head. The swishing sound it made as it ripped through the air caused him to look over his shoulder. C.J. saw his utter surprise as he spied her towering over him, wild-eyed, her brown hair flying, huge white bandages on her hands and swinging a Chinese mallet. He stared, slack-jawed, as the weapon hit its target perfectly.

The man's whole body seemed to vibrate, then crumpled to the floor.

The other man noticed the commotion and turned his head just long enough for Darius to land a crushing blow to his momentarily unprotected jaw.

Darius and C.J. backed toward the window. He raised his eyebrows and looked at her. She raised hers and returned his glance. Slowly, a smile crept across his face, her lips curving upward in response. How astounding, she thought, as she looked at her captors lying on the floor.

Then, grinning smugly, she and Darius crawled out the window and escaped.

CHAPTER 9

*D*arius unlocked the door to C.J.'s hotel room and walked in. She was sitting in her bed, leaning against a pile of pillows, with the covers pulled up around her neck. A short while earlier she had cleansed the blisters on her hands and had changed into a very unsexy cotton nightgown—the only kind she owned.

"Room service will bring up your order as soon as possible," he said, broad smile on his face. "And I found some ointment and bandages for your hands."

He perched on the edge of the bed, dipped two fingers into the jar of the greasy, healing balm and held her hands as if they were fragile porcelain while he smeared ointment on them.

"I think you could use a little of that yourself," she said, eyeing a red mark on his jaw and his slightly scraped knuckles.

"No, I'll be fine. And you will, too." He covered not only the areas of her hands with blisters, but her entire palm and fingers. She wasn't about to complain or correct him. No one had ever tried to help her that way since she was a little kid, and even then, her mother usually just handed her Bactine when she had a scrape or cut.

"At least I learned what 'C.J.' stands for," he said as he meticulously covered both hands.

She looked puzzled. "You did?"

"Yep. Calamity Jane."

She laughed. "Very funny! I don't even know how many days I was there, and you make jokes about it!"

"Days?" It was his turn to chuckle as he finished his ministration. "Four or five hours are more like it."

"That's all? I thought it was an eternity!" Her eyes softened as she looked at him. "Thank you for finding me. I was dumb to go there, and deep down, I knew it even as I got into the car with those two men. I should learn to listen to my gut reaction."

"Or mine. As I recall, I did warn you." With a feather-soft touch he brushed her hair away from her brow, and tucked a lock of it behind her ear.

"Saying 'I told you so' is not an admirable characteristic, Mr. Kane. I feel bad enough already."

"You're right." He nodded. "Enough said."

"But how did you find me?"

He scowled. "It wasn't hard. When I couldn't find you, I figured Alan had talked you into going back to Yeng's. Your brother's a bigger menace than I thought!"

"He wouldn't knowingly send me into danger."

Darius shut his eyes for a moment, as if to stop the retort he was ready to give. "Let's hope you're right. Anyway, there was quite a bit of activity around Yeng's place. Then, late in the afternoon, he and most of the others left, which gave me a chance to sneak in."

She gasped as he suddenly grabbed her shoulders. "If you ever do anything so dangerous again," he shouted, "it won't be Yeng you'll have to worry about! It'll be me. Why won't you listen to me?"

The timbre of his voice told her how hurt he had been by her lack of trust in him. She longed to take his hands, but she couldn't—hers were too greasy. Instead, she proceeded to tell him the whole story of her conversation with Alan, of meeting the two men outside the city prison, and then of telling Yeng about Chan Li.

Room service arrived. A bacon, lettuce and tomato club sandwich with a cup of clam chowder helped her to feel considerably more at peace with the world. She wiped some of the ointment off her fingertips so she could eat. Darius didn't say anything else until her meal had ended and she was sipping a cup of coffee.

"Alan was released today," he said finally.

"Released? Really?" She stared at him and he nodded. "That's wonderful! But now I'm even more confused. Yeng said he was going to see that Alan was released, and it seems he did. But why would he lock me up?"

"I'm not so sure it was Yeng, C.J. I doubt he has any influence with British Intelligence, and they're the ones who were holding Alan."

"Why, then, was he released?"

"I don't know. All I can say is that the next step is Alan's."

"It is?" Her mind was spinning. Had Yeng gotten Alan released? Or, if he hadn't done it, who had? And why?

"One way or the other," Darius said, "Alan is the key to everything."

A chill swept over her. "I see."

"He'll try to contact you here eventually, and I suspect Yeng's men will be watching your every move."

"Great. Now I'm a prisoner in my own hotel room."

"It's not that bad."

"You don't have to stay here. I'll be fine."

"I don't mind staying with you."

"Really? In that case, got a pack of cards?" She gave a half-hearted smile. "I'm a whiz at gin rummy."

He eyed her. "I've got a better idea, Cinderella. Tonight your pumpkin turns into a coach."

She was puzzled. "But I thought—"

"We won't be able to leave the hotel, but it has a restaurant and even a cocktail lounge with a dance floor. What do you say? Does it sound like fun?"

Fun and then some, she thought. Did she dare go? She could stay here and rest, but she knew she wouldn't sleep. She could stay and worry about Alan, but that wouldn't help. Knowing him, she half expected him to call and say British intelligence realized their mistake and he was going back to the Peace Corps in Sarawak.

"All right," she said, surprised that her voice sounded so breathless. "Let's do it."

"Great." He stood. "I'll change into something more presentable. Maybe even a tie and dinner jacket. I'll be back in no time." Then his eyes narrowed. "But first, promise me that if Alan calls and has another bright idea, you will not leave this room without me."

"Okay."

"I mean it, C.J." She had already learned that when he called her

C.J. he was deadly serious. "If I return," he continued, "and you're gone, I will personally wring your neck. Do you under—"

"Yes, yes, yes. Now get out of here."

He looked as if he wanted to speak, but he didn't. Instead, he quickly turned and left.

She placed her fingertips against her lips as she watched the door close behind him. In a moment she threw back the covers and jumped off the bed. She had so much to do to get ready.

She ran to the closet: two slacks, one skirt, three blouses, and only one dress, a practical rust-colored synthetic no-wrinkle sundress. Her heart sank. Packing for the jungles of Sarawak just didn't include glad rags. As she reached for the hanger, being careful not to touch the dress itself with her greasy hands, she realized that she didn't own the kind of clothes she would want to wear on a date with Darius.

She had to wash her hair, do her nails. She looked down at her hands and suddenly felt dizzy.

All her excitement dissipated as quickly as it had appeared. The terrors of the day came flooding back, and she abruptly sat on the edge of the bed again, still holding her hands out in front of her.

What am I doing? she wondered.

She carefully washed the ointment off her palms, reapplied only small dabs on the blisters and then covered them with bandaids. She leaned forward, her heart pounding, trying to recover her composure.

She reached for an emery board and began methodically trying to salvage something from the mess her nails had become. As she worked, her breathing returned to normal.

Darius would be back soon; she had to pull herself together. She wondered what he would look like in a tie and dinner jacket—probably like a caged animal. The idea was incongruous. Darius belonged outdoors; he belonged where a man could be free to live by his wits and his strength. He was as wild as the jungle, and she loved him for it.

Loved him? No, she shook her head, not love. She was fascinated, intrigued. Maybe even a bit in lust. Who was she kidding? There was no maybe about it.

But not love. She wasn't the type to fall in love, and she definitely wasn't the type others fell in love with. As the years passed, she had become ever more accepting of her solitary existence.

Yet if she were the type to fall in love, it would be with someone like Darius.

She put down the nail file, surprised at how her hand was shaking, then headed for the shower.

She dried her hair, took special care with her makeup, and was applying a dab of cologne when she heard a knock at the door. Darius called out, "It's me."

Pulling her robe tightly around her, she opened the door.

How could I have been so wrong? was the first thought that came to her. The second was that she should shut her mouth, because she must look ridiculous with it gaping open.

"May I come in?" Darius asked, standing in the door way.

She stepped aside, still speechless. To think that she had imagined he would look out of place in a dinner jacket. The obviously expensive jacket was light gray, worn with slacks in a darker shade. His shirt was white, and the tie blended pink and gray in diagonal stripes.

His tan was even more striking than it was with his usual, sportier clothes. The golden ends of his hair curled lazily around the collar of the shirt, and his eyes were captivating as ever.

"Is anything wrong?" he asked.

She shook her head.

"Well, then, charming as you are standing there in that robe, unless you'd like me in a similar state of undress, I suggest you put some clothes on."

She looked down at herself. "Oh! Please, sit down. I'll just be a minute."

She took her dress into the bathroom and finished getting ready. The sleeveless dress had a simple V neckline, a long sash around the waist, and hugged her full figure.

As she stepped into the room, Darius stood, his eyes shining as he drank in the soft material that emphasized the curve of her breasts, her waist and inviting hips.

"Maybe you are Cinderella! You look beautiful." His voice was quiet, intense.

She felt herself blush at his compliment, wanting, but not daring, to believe him. No one had ever accused her of being beautiful before.

"Here, I brought this for you," he said.

C.J. hadn't even noticed the small box he had been carrying as he entered the room.

"Oh, Darius," was all she could say when she opened it.

Inside was an orchid, a blend of orange, yellow and rust— exactly the same shade as her dress. Her gaze lifted to his.

"Thank you," she said quietly, running her finger over the soft petals. "I don't think I've ever gotten one of these before."

"The men you knew were really blind, C.J."

She searched his eyes, expecting to see that he was joking, but his expression was that of a man looking at a woman he admired. Her throat tightened, and she dropped her gaze, flustered.

"Here," he said, taking the orchid in his hand. "Let me help you." He stepped close to her, the heady, masculine scent of his after shave filling the air. "Hmm," he said, "where should it go?" He turned the corsage this way and that in the vicinity of her shoulder.

"Right here." She pointed to a spot on the shoulder of her dress. "This way." She turned the orchid right side up, brushing his hand with hers as she did so. She scarcely breathed.

The heat of his fingers against her skin caused a quick intake of her breath. Quickly, she clasped her hands behind her back, not trusting them with him so near.

"Thank you," she said, having trouble regaining her voice.

He didn't step back, but he did move his hand from the neckline of the dress to her neck, then ran his finger along her throat, then upward.

She stood rigid, scarcely breathing.

His eyes bored into her, studying her face. His expression filled with tenderness as he dropped his hand. "I told the desk clerk where we'd be, so if Alan calls, they'll be able to find you," he said.

Alan. Of course. She couldn't allow herself to forget that Darius's main—probably only—reason for being here was Alan to track down the White Dragon and claim the reward. She nodded.

"I'm sure he's all right," Darius said as they headed for the elevator.

At the far corner of the lobby, near the main entrance to the hotel, hidden behind a partition of ferns and lattice- work, was a cocktail lounge. A lonesome piano stood in the corner.

Darius led C.J. to a small table. The bar was empty, except for the two of them and the bartender.

"This is nice," C.J. said. "The ferns remind me of a place near my apartment called Muldoon's. Thursday nights they serve a great pasta spread. I usually go. It breaks up the monotony of the week."

"Muldoon's sells pasta in a fern bar?"

"It's L.A." C.J. shrugged.

Chuckling, Darius walked to the bar to order a whiskey sour for her and scotch on the rocks for himself. When he returned to the table, she pointed at the piano in the corner. The combo hadn't yet shown up.

"I'm sure no one will mind if you play something."

He grinned. "You know me and pianos. Once I start, you have to pry me loose from the keys."

"So play." She touched his hand. "Play something for me. Please?"

He placed his other hand on top of hers and squeezed gently.

"If that's what you want." He got up and spoke briefly to the bartender. C.J. saw the man nod and shrug in a way that indicated he couldn't care less. Darius sat down at the piano, looked at her and winked.

He played a medley of popular tunes, *If Ever I Would Leave You, Love Look Away, A Time For Us,* and ending with *Somewhere* from *West Side Story.* The songs were beautiful and sad, and Darius played with all the emotional intensity the work deserved. People came into the bar as his playing progressed, not to drink, but to listen.

When he stopped, they applauded warmly. He looked shocked. He'd been concentrating so intently on the music that he hadn't even been aware when they entered.

"Encore!" they clamored, but Darius thanked them, shook his head and joined C.J.

She smiled at him. "That was beautiful. I love the way you play," she whispered.

"I'm glad, Carina. Now, how about some dinner?"

She nodded as he led her from the lounge.

"Hey, fella," the bartender called as they walked toward the exit, "anytime you want a job here, see me. We could use some class."

"Thanks," Darius said. "I'll remember."

Past the cocktail lounge was the restaurant. A waiter showed them to a table by the window.

"Tell me," she said, in an offhanded way. "Do you own a piano?"

"Sure." He opened the menu and began studying it.

She opened hers. "Where is it?"

"Pretty sneaky way to ask where I live, isn't it?" he said without looking up.

She peered over the top of the menu. "Now, why would I want to know such a thing?"

He smiled. "The piano is at my parents' home in Massachusetts, just outside Boston."

"I see." She dropped her gaze and began to study the menu, and she didn't look at him as she spoke. "Do you go there often?"

"Nope."

"Too busy?"

"Nope."

"Just don't want to?"

He shut his menu and took her hand, careful of the bandaids. "I rarely see them anymore, all right?" He paused, and then more words tumbled from his lips. "I also have a daughter, and an ex-wife, and I never see them either." His voice was soft as he spoke.

C.J. felt as if her heart had stopped beating. She tried not to show her shock as she removed her hand from his, unfolded her napkin, and placed it on her lap. Then she picked up the menu again and opened it, her eyes downcast. "A daughter?" she said. "How old is she?"

"Five and a half."

She paused. "And you don't get to see her?"

"I don't see her." He sat back in his seat, his expression enigmatic and very far away. "Her name is Alicia. In pictures, she's a pretty little girl, black hair like her mother, and big green eyes like her old man. But the situation..." He stopped speaking.

She caught his eye. "Like the situation that causes you to drift around Asia?"

"I don't want to talk about it." The pain in his words was palpable.

"We never talk about you, Darius. We blither on about me for hours. And Alan—we go on and on about him. I want to know about you."

"I've heard the prime rib here is very good. But if you're interested in shellfish, the lobster comes highly recommended."

She sighed, shutting her menu and laying it aside. "Prime rib. Medium rare."

He placed his menu on top of hers. "A woman after my own heart."

A slight grin came to her lips. You got out of that one, Darius Kane, she thought, but someday I'll get you to talk. Someday you'll understand how much I want to know.

They ordered dinner and Cabernet Sauvignon. The combo began to play *Twelfth of Never.* "Let's dance," Darius suggested.

On the dance floor, as much as C.J. liked his nearness, his arm around her, her hand in his, the few sentences he'd said about his past had made her realize how little she knew him. He had an ex-wife and a child. The thought kept going round and round in her mind, blotting out everything else. There was so much she wanted to know, but didn't dare ask. She had no right to ask. She was nothing to him; it was none of her business, but still…

Darius sighed and stopped dancing. She looked up at him in confusion.

"Come on, Clytemnestra," he said, leading her back to the table, the sound of resignation heavy in his voice.

"But the dance…"

He led her back to the table without saying anything else.

"What's the matter?" she asked as they sat.

"Don't look so innocent. You know exactly what's wrong." His jaw was firmly set, and his eyes showed no emotion as he began to speak. "I've been divorced for five years. I have never regretted getting the divorce, and I still don't. My only regret is not seeing Alicia. It's easy on her; she was just a baby when I left. Her mother has since remarried twice, so Alicia's had her share of surrogate fathers. Not that it's right. Not at all. Sometimes it hurts like hell when I let myself think about her."

"You don't have to tell me—"

"It seems I do."

She held her breath, anxious over what she might hear.

He paused for a moment. "My ex-wife lives in New York City, so if you think I'm still carrying a torch for her, or vice versa, give her a call. Her name is Nadia Balensky. You may have heard of her."

C.J. felt a shock ripple through her. "Not the violinist?"

"One and the same."

She was speechless. His ex-wife was talented, wealthy and beautiful. Darius was clearly the kind of man who could attract and marry such a woman. If he could have a Nadia Balensky, why would he give a second glance to a C.J. Perkins? The answer was obvious; he wouldn't. But then, the whole idea of the two of them together was preposterous anyway. She fought the urge to leave, to go back to her hotel room alone. "I see."

"No, you don't see. My relationship with Nadia is over. Finished. It's something I wouldn't even talk about except when an interesting young woman decides to write me out of her life because I made the mistake of once having been divorced."

Her cheeks reddened. "I'm not…I mean…" She looked up at him. "Maybe I was." He seemed to be hanging on her every word. But surely, she was misreading him. She shook her head. "I'm sorry. Here I was thinking of you as someone who sprang full-grown from the jungle like a modern day Tarzan, and instead I learn you're more like Henry the Eighth."

He grinned. "One ex-wife, not six and she's still got her head. At this stage, I might add, I no longer regret it!"

"Good," she said.

He stroked his chin. "Tarzan, is it? Then you must be my Jane."

Her eyes widened in surprise.

"Jane! Aha! That's it, isn't it? There's no other reason for you to look so startled, like a kid with her hand in the cookie jar. Jane. I'm right, aren't I?" He took a sip of wine, his eyes never leaving hers. "I guess we're telling all our secrets tonight."

"Okay, you guessed that one." She grinned.

"And the C?" He raised one eyebrow.

"A girl's got to keep some mystery, you know," she replied.

As Darius had promised, the dinner was excellent. After dinner, they returned to the cocktail lounge for martinis. The combo played lots of ballads, a few cha-chas, all up beat and light. Darius pulled her onto the dance floor. He was an excellent dancer, as she had expected. He was the kind of dancer any woman loved to be with, one so good, he made her feel light and graceful.

She could have stayed in his arms forever.

"Someday," he said as they danced, "I'd like to really take you out on the town. San Francisco's a lot of fun at night. I wish I could show it to you."

"I wish you could, too. Maybe, when this is over."

"I know, Carmelita. I know." With that, he held her closer and laid his cheek against her hair. She shut her eyes, shut away everything except the bliss of holding him..

A short while later she was surprised to hear the alto sax player announce the last dance, *My Funny Valentine.*

"Already?" She looked at her watch. "I'm so turned around by the time, I don't know if it's night or day anymore."

He smiled and wrapped her in his arms again. It felt too good to be with him, and there was danger in that. Danger to her well-protected heart.

He'll go away soon, she told herself as they danced. Back to that strange existence he was living in Hong Kong. She felt it as surely as she knew her own name: one day he would leave her. But that's what you want him to do, she reminded herself. Exactly what you want.

"Time to go," he said as the music ended.

She let her arms fall to her sides. "Yes. Alan hasn't called yet, either. I guess I'll be awake all night waiting for the telephone to ring."

He grinned. "Want company?"

Her stomach tightened, and her heartbeat quickened. She could say that she would prefer to be alone, but she didn't. She wanted to be with him.

"Sure." She answered with a measured casualness she didn't feel. "A nightcap sounds fine."

Darius went in search of some refreshments after seeing C.J. to her room, but came back a short while later with only two cans of soda. He handed her one. "Everything's closed. I was lucky to find a soda machine with something still in it."

"This is fine," she said, settling into a chair.

He took off his jacket and tie, tossed them onto the arm of a chair, then unbuttoned the top button of his shirt and rolled up the sleeves to just below the elbow. Every gesture exuded male sexuality, and she couldn't stop watching him.

"So tell me more about yourself, C. Jane Perkins," he said as he sat on the bed and sipped his soda. "You're from Ohio, right?"

"Columbus. I went to Ohio State, studied art, then I moved to L.A. What about you?"

"Juilliard. Piano."

"I see." She paused. "Then what?"

The easygoing grin had vanished as his gaze lifted to hers, and he hesitated, as if deciding whether to joke, or give a real answer. "I traveled, went to Europe, gave concerts. The usual thing for an aspiring pianist. There were competitions and classes. Lots of classes. And endless hours of practice. I could have jogged around the world three times in all the time I wasted practicing."

"It wasn't wasted, Darius. Not the way you play." Her heart went out to him.

He said nothing.

She leaned forward. "Tell me what happened."

His green eyes darkened with pain before he dropped them, saying nothing. *Stop hurting so, Darius,* she wanted to cry, but instead, she hurried on, almost babbling. "Do you realize it's hardly been a week since we met? We've been together so much, been through so much, I feel I should know you as well as I know myself, but really, I hardly know you at all."

A flicker of curiosity crossed his face.

"I want to know you better," she continued, almost whispering as she added, "I want to know everything about you." Her cheeks burned with embarrassment as she realized how much her statement had revealed. She rubbed her forehead. "Forget that. I never should have said that."

"Why not?" His face remained serious. "It was honest. And, I have to admit, flattering."

She abruptly stood and hurried over to the windows so she could look out, so she could look anywhere but at him. The fog must have been hovering somewhere out over the Pacific Ocean, because the night was clear, and C.J. could see the city in all its splendor, shimmering far below them.

"What's wrong?" he asked.

She stiffened at his words, despite their truth. She could easily make a fool of herself over this man. She wouldn't let that happen. More than anything, she wanted to say something clever, witty, sophisticated, but all she could do was clutch her arms tightly and try to control her surging emotions. She forced her voice to sound lilting and casual as she faced him. "Nothing."

He waited a long moment before he said softly, "Why don't I believe you?" His voice grew gentle. "What are you trying to avoid, Chloe?"

"Stop calling me those silly names!"

"What are you running from?"

"Nothing!"

He stood in front of her. "Me?"

"Of course not!"

"Your independence? Or is it just your dependence?"

"I have no idea what you're talking about." She clamped her lips together in defiance.

"Don't you? Tell me, why were you the one, alone, searching the backwaters of Asia trying to find your brother? Is your father too old? Too sick? What?" he demanded, taking hold of her hands.

She froze, then pulled herself from his grasp, putting some space between them before she faced him again. "My father is fine. And it was quite natural that I'd be the one to look for Alan. I'm always the one who does things in my family!"

"Everyone depends on C.J., and C.J. depends on no one. I see. So that's why you get feisty instead of grateful when someone tries to help you."

"I'm never—"

"Sometimes downright ornery."

"Where did you learn that Southwest drivel if you're really from Massachusetts?"

"Suspicious, too," he said, his eyes sparkling as he moved ever closer to her. "And totally untrusting."

"I am not," she said breathlessly, grasping his shoulders both to steady herself and to hold him back.

"Contradictory." He put his hands on her waist.

"I'm never contradictory." Tingles cascading down her back met with ripples running up it.

"Contrary." His eyes met hers.

"Darius!"

"And far too talkative."

As their gazes locked, any protest she might have uttered died unspoken.

His expression turned suddenly serious, and her pulse raced in response. She felt a hardening of his muscles beneath her hands as his gaze captured hers. He slowly pulled her closer.

"No!" She pushed him away even as her senses warred against her, and then turned and took a few steps to regain her sanity. Dangerous Kane, she thought, you make my mind and body seem like strangers to me, with an unbending will all their own. "This is crazy!"

"Crazy? I think it's the sanest thing I've done since I first met you," he replied. "Do you have any idea what it was like that first morning in Hong Kong after sleeping in your bed, smelling your perfume all night, and then waking up with you curled there beside me?"

"No—."

"Or worse," he interrupted, once more closing the gap between them, "leaving you lying in my bed at the Mark just last night?"

Her words caught in her throat.

"You," he whispered, his hands cupped her face, "are a beautiful, desirable woman."

She wanted to believe him, wanted it desperately. But she couldn't. She spent a life knowing she wasn't pretty, desirable, or anything else he was implying. She was klutzy, inexperienced C.J. She never had a lover. She could have, especially in her college years. But the guys who were interested, she didn't care for, and those she cared about weren't interested. So she'd waited. Waited for a love that never came.

And now, if she were to give in to what she wanted, he would find out…and how completely pathetic she would seem to him!

"Don't patronize me!" she said between clenched teeth.

He dropped his hands, giving up. "There's something good between us, Cleo. As much as you try to ignore it, you know there is. You feel it every bit as much as I do."

She folded her arms. "Fun's fun, but we have work to do," she tried to keep her voice light, uncaring. "I don't want another lover. And we can't lose track of what we're here for—to help my brother. So, if you want sex, look elsewhere, and I'll do the same."

He stepped back as if slapped. "I'm not looking for 'sex.' Clearly, I misread you. I apologize."

She turned her head away from his, unable to meet the soft green eyes that seemed to penetrate to her soul. "I like everything just the way it is." She couldn't look at him, couldn't allow herself to realize how strongly she felt about him. How much she wanted him. "Go back to your hotel, jungle man." She walked to the door and opened it for him. "It's late. You're raving."

"You never cease to surprise me, Cleo. You never do." With a shake of his head, he left.

She shut the door and then leaned against it as if to force herself not to fling it open, to throw herself at him. She drew in a shuddering breath.

"My God," she whispered as the morning with Alan, the afternoon in Yeng's cellar and the evening with Darius drifted through her thoughts. "For a girl from Columbus, what a day!"

CHAPTER 11

*S*he couldn't ignore the loud ringing in her ears, and realized it was her telephone. The early light of morning brightened the room.

"Hello?" She was surprised to find that her voice worked.

"It's me," said the quiet voice on the other end.

She clutched the phone and sat up. "Alan!"

"C.J., I need your help." Alan sounded desperate.

"Where are you?"

"I'm…I don't know. It doesn't matter. I can't stay here. I've got to go. I've got to run."

"Run? What do you mean, 'run'? What's going on?" she cried.

"I can't explain now. Meet me."

"Sure. Where?"

"There's a big old movie house called the Empire on Market and Eighth. It opens at noon. Buy a ticket and go to the balcony, top row. I'll be there."

"Okay, but—"

A soft click told her that the connection had been broken.

"Alan? Alan?" As she placed the receiver back into its cradle, the realization that Alan hadn't told her the truth about any of this settled over her, filling her with despair and worry.

Almost immediately, she heard a knock on her door.

"What's wrong?" Darius said by way of greeting. He wore light gray slacks, a close-fitting black pullover, and his leather jacket. He was truly a man of surprises.

"Good morning to you, too." She raked her fingers through her hair. "I must look wretched," she said.

"Not to me."

"Why are you here?" she demanded.

"I think it's for the same reason I see a worried frown on your face," he replied. "I figured that since Alan didn't contact you last night, he'd try this morning, or not at all. I take it, he must have called you."

She saw the concern in his eyes. Although she knew that his real goal was the bounty on the White Dragon, still, in some crazy, inexplicable way, he was the only one who helped her, who comforted her, and who was there for her to lean on. For that she was grateful, and for so much more. Later, she would be strong again. Later, she would take on the whole world if she had to—and do it alone, as always. Later, she would be practical again. But not now.

She reached out to touch his hand. "Sometimes I think you're the only one who's been right about any of this. Thank you for being here. For helping me."

He stared at her then, as if stunned by her heart-felt comments.

She wished she could take them back, hating that she revealed as much of herself to him. She had never done that with anyone. "Of course," she said finally, falling back on her old flippancy. "I'm sure you're that way with all your women."

"All my women?" He grinned. "I'd like to know where they are. I've been missing something."

"There must be at least a half dozen in Hong Kong alone."

"Sorry to disappoint you. The only one who cares about me in Hong Kong is Jimmy Lee. And I assure you, it's not physical."

She smiled. "Good. Anyway, I've got to shower, dress, eat something and then meet Alan downtown at noon."

"That sounds fine. I haven't eaten yet either."

"You aren't going with me."

"Of course I am."

As she picked up her clothes and headed for the shower, thoughts of being locked in Yeng's basement came back to her and she had to admit she was glad for his words. "Okay," she whispered.

San Francisco lent itself perfectly to walking. Like Hong Kong, it was hilly and offered beautiful views of the water. Casually, they strolled through the streets to a small coffee shop off Union Square where they had a light breakfast. They spent time wandering through the downtown area until the Market Street movie house opened.

"I didn't steal the jade," Alan said.

"That's obvious. It was a well-planned, very professional job," Darius replied.

"But I know where it is."

"That, too, is very clear."

C.J. glowered at Darius. "Let him tell his story."

"All right, Perkins." Darius ignored C.J.'s angry look and concentrated on Alan. "From the beginning."

C.J. looked from one man to the other. She and Darius were sitting in the back row of the theater, Alan directly in front of them. The two most important men in her life had taken one look at each other and instantly flashed hostile.

Maybe it was just the circumstances under which they had met, or the poisonous atmosphere in the bleak theater, that caused their ill feelings she thought hopefully. The theater was old and enormous, the kind that showed third-rate features to an audience of winos who needed to come in from the cold and teenagers who needed a warm place to make out.

As the two men warily eyed each other, C.J. thought how ironic it was. Alan needed Darius to help him out of this situation. Darius needed Alan to get the jade, yet both pretended to be there because of her. Darius had made it clear to her that, since his accident, the search for treasure and the rewards of finding it were what gave him purpose.

Alan coughed slightly, his eyes shifting from one to the other.

"I want the truth," Darius said coldly.

"I know, but. . ." He looked around. "It'll take time. They might find us."

"Listen, Perkins!"

"All right! I'll tell you.... It started the way I told C.J. Did she tell you?"

"She gave me your version of events. We both know there was a lot you didn't explain to her."

"Well,"—Alan sounded embarrassed—"as I said, I was in Malaysia, on the beach, and in the distance I spotted something. I moved closer and saw it was a man. He'd been washed up, and was half dead."

Darius leaned back in his chair and eyed Alan suspiciously. Alan noticed. "I know it sounds crazy. But it's true! Look at me. I'm not the kind of person to get mixed up in an international jade theft, except by accident. It was a crazy accident that, God knows, I wish had never happened!"

"That's true enough." Darius grimaced. "Go on."

"The man could barely speak, but he wanted desperately to talk. He knew he was dying. He knew his friends had been murdered. He told me a tale that made my blood run cold. He had to tell it."

C.J. nodded encouragingly, willing him on, believing in his innocence.

"He was... I guess we'd call him a pirate. He and his friends were hired by a man named Chan Li."

"Chan Li?" C.J. interrupted. "You mean Mr. Yeng's friend?"

Alan looked sheepish. "They aren't friends. I knew Yeng would recognize Chan Li as the man who stole the White Dragon, and when he heard the name, he'd know I have the Dragon now."

"What!" Darius leaned forward and grabbed the front of Alan's shirt. C.J. sat unmoving, shocked by Alan's words. "You sent your own sister to Yeng spouting the name of a man like that!"

Alan made a whimpering sound as he tried to free himself. C.J. reached out and took Darius's arm, although her mind and heart reeled with the knowledge that Alan had lied to her.

"Please," she said.

Darius let go with a shove, then glared at C.J. "He's not worth saving."

"I'm sorry! I didn't realize…" Alan mewled.

Darius snorted. C.J. remained silent as Alan continued his tale, but she couldn't get rid of the sick feeling that had filled her.

"The pirate explained to me that Chan Li lived in Luchow, near Hong Kong. He was an underworld figure, a thief, and had come up with a way to steal the White Dragon. He needed help, however, and that's where the pirates came in. They thought they were partners with Chan Li, but he had a very different plan in mind.

"They stole the jade, and Chan Li hid it behind the face of an antique grandfather clock he had. It had a secret compartment that looked like it housed clock workings—springs and all, but instead it was hollow. He even showed the pirates how the compartment worked."

"Because he knew the pirates would never live to open it?" C.J. asked.

"That's right." Alan nervously eyed Darius before continuing.

"Chan Li gave the pirates a sealed container they believed contained the Dragon. They were to carry it to Singapore, where Chan Li said he would meet them, and then sell it to his connections and split the proceeds. But in the middle of the South China Sea, a hidden bomb caused the boat to blow up.

"My pirate was the only one to survive the bomb, and he realized Chan Li had duped them. He got onto a raft, and it brought him to the island. He knew he was dying. I was his only hope of getting even with Chan Li, so he told me where to find the White Dragon and how to open the grandfather clock's secret compartment. Soon after that, he died."

"And then?" Darius asked impatiently.

"I went to Luchow and found Chan Li's house. I hid, watching it for several days, hoping to find it empty at some point. Then, one night, something strange happened. Lights were on, but there was no movement whatsoever.

"I sneaked up to the house. It was unguarded, so I entered. What I saw was so horrible it still gives me nightmares. A bodyguard was dead, shot to death, just beyond the doorway, and a little farther into the house was another. Then, in the main room, I found Chan Li, his blood splattered around him.

"The rooms had all been torn apart. Even the grandfather clock had been knocked on its side and the workings torn out of it, but no one tore into the unit that housed them. So, although the face had been smashed, the secret compartment wasn't discovered. I opened it the way the pirate had said, and inside lay the White Dragon. I grabbed it and was out of the house in a matter of minutes.

"I had planned on turning everything over to the police the next day. But then I started thinking. The reward would be big, but Chan Li would have sold the jade for more. And, I figured, his buyer must be in Hong Kong since he didn't try to smuggle the jade out of the area.

"So I hid the Dragon in the only place I knew where it would be absolutely safe for a long time. Then I started to leave little hints here and there around Hong Kong, clues, to indicate that if anyone was interested in the jade, they should talk to me. No one did."

Alan sighed before continuing. "People were afraid because of Chan Li's murder. Everyone knew he was connected with the theft. He had become wealthy by smuggling goods in and out of Communist China. That's why he lived in Luchow near the border."

"Wait," Darius interrupted. "Where did you learn that?"

"I don't remember. It just seemed to be general knowledge."

"I see," Darius said thoughtfully.

C.J. looked from one to the other. She didn't fully understand what was going on, but she didn't want to interrupt.

"Well, anyway," Alan said, "a few people mentioned a wealthy man living in San Francisco named Yeng. They indicated that he might be interested in the jade. I was getting more and more nervous in Hong Kong, so I decided to play it safe. I went to San Francisco.

"I was picked up by the police as soon as I stepped off the plane. The Brits in Hong Kong had contacted them, expecting I'd show up at the airport. I hired a lawyer, who said my situation sounded dismal—something about a paper connecting me, the Dragon and Luchow."

"I'm sorry, Alan," C.J. said. "It must have been the note I found in your room. I showed it to a number of officials, starting in Singapore. Now I know why none of them would answer my questions about it."

"It's not your fault," Alan said bleakly.

"Why didn't you just go to Yeng when you were released from jail?" Darius asked.

"It was because of something C.J. told me you said—that Yeng was dangerous. I didn't want to believe it, but you were right. I had stupidly hoped Yeng would be some honest, trustworthy fellow willing to spend close to a million dollars for a very hot Chinese artifact. Who was I kidding? Even the people who told me about him never said he was a nice guy. Getting involved in all this, God, I was a fool!"

"Um hmm," Darius murmured in agreement.

C.J. gave him a scathing look.

Alan continued, ignoring them both. "I don't know why the police let me go. I don't know if it was due to Yeng, or if the British decided they had nothing to hold me on, or what. I went to Yeng's house and watched the kind of people who went in and out of it. They're gangsters, no doubt about it. I'm afraid of Yeng, of him finding me. My sending him the name Chan Li could be my death sentence. I sent it thinking he would want to negotiate, but I'm afraid negotiating wouldn't be on his mind. Now that he knows I have the jade, all he has to do is find me, and force me to tell him where to find it."

"Oh, Alan." C.J. grabbed his hands in hers.

He pulled his back as soon as he felt the bandages. "God, C.J., what did you do to yourself?"

"Leave her alone, Perkins," Darius said with a snarl. "You'll have to disappear. It's your only hope. You don't want to take the chance of falling into Yeng's hands."

"That's what I was afraid of. Thank God it's a big country. I had better get started. C.J., do you have any money? I spent most of mine."

She pulled out her purse. "I've only got about a hundred and fifty dollars in cash."

"That'll do for a start," he said, reaching for it all, to her astonishment. "What would I do without you?"

She turned instinctively to Darius for help. "I've got money; don't worry," he murmured, then gave Alan a look of scorn.

C.J.'s gaze went from one man to the other; she was unable to stop comparing them, and her eyes rested with both hurt and disappointment on her brother.

Alan raised his chin under this double scrutiny, a petulant bend to his lips as he turned to Darius. "You don't like me, do you, Kane?"

"No. But I'm trying to ignore that for C.J.'s sake. What I can't ignore is that you haven't told us where the Dragon is now."

"Oh, yes, the Dragon." He fidgeted.

"Tell us," Darius said, his voice low. "You'll never be safe from Yeng until he knows it's no longer in your hands."

"God," Alan moaned.

"Alan!" C.J. cried, hardly able to believe his reluctance.

"All right! It's in Sarawak."

"Sarawak!" C.J. and Darius exclaimed in unison.

"Sure. I didn't know where else to hide it, and with my Peace Corps credentials I could come and go with no problem. So I went back to Sarawak. I didn't go to my old village—that would have caused too many questions. Instead I rented a car in Kuching and drove to an area near my old village, but I made sure no one saw me out there. I buried the jade in the jungle, in the middle of nothing, a good three hours from any dwellings. From there, I went back to Hong Kong…and you know the rest of the story."

"Once the jade is returned to the Chinese government," Darius said, "Yeng will stop pursuing you. You need to draw us a map. We'll get the Dragon and turn it in, and you'll be a free man. Just one thing: C.J. and I split the reward money, fifty-fifty."

C.J. looked at him in shock, feeling as if she'd just been doused with a pail of cold water. Darius wanted the reward money; how could she have forgotten that? But then, if he could find the jade and allow her brother to be safe, he deserved every penny of it.

Her jaw tight, she handed Alan a small notepad, and he proceeded to draw.

He sketched guideposts and gave explanations as he did. It took nearly ten minutes. "That should do it. It's kind of hard to describe jungle. One reason it's such a good hiding place is that it's all so similar." He shook his head, then smiled weakly. "Good luck, you two. Don't spend all that loot in one place." His eyes met his sister's. "I'm sorry, C.J. I hope, someday, you'll forgive me."

Then Alan was gone.

C.J. trembled as thoughts swirled of what Alan had done, of his selfish disregard for the law and for her. Darius watched her, not sure what to do to ease her unhappiness. "Do you want to go now?" he asked.

"Yes, please." She hardly recognized her own voice.

"Let's get out of here." He led her from the theater. "We can walk back to your hotel from here."

The fog they had watched roll in earlier now blanketed the city, and they huddled close together as they walked.

"I'm going with you, you know," she said, her jaw set.

"Of course. It's your hotel room."

"You know what I mean," she said.

"If by that you mean to Sarawak, the answer is no."

"It wasn't a question, and I am going! He's my brother."

"C.J., trekking through the jungle looking for buried treasure is not the kind of thing you can do. You have no training, no stamina. Believe me, it's not like in the movies. Sarawak is infested with dangerous insects and snakes—not to mention leopards. Even the monkeys aren't the cute, friendly little creatures you see on television. They can turn into ferocious, biting, clawing monsters if you upset a tribe of them."

Her stomach tightened at his description. "Nonsense. Alan went in there alone, and he got out again very easily. If he can do it, certainly the two of us together can."

"He lived there for three years. He knew exactly what he was doing. You were only in the village for a few days. Do you remember what the jungle was like beyond that village? Do you remember the nights there, when you lay in your bed and heard animal cries and strange noises you couldn't begin to understand in the darkness? The jungle comes alive at night, and it can be very, very frightening."

"Stop! I'm going with you, no matter what you say. I don't appreciate you trying to frighten me like this."

"You still don't trust me, do you?"

She felt herself pale slightly as his words hit home. Still, she couldn't be sure how much of her insistence on going was because of a lack of trust, and how much was because she hated the thought of not being with him. She jutted out her chin. "Of course I trust you. Otherwise, I wouldn't go with you. I'd find someone else to take me!"

"If you trusted me, you'd go to Hong Kong and wait. Why don't you go to Jimmy's. I'll meet you there."

"How can you meet me in Hong Kong? I thought the police were after you. In fact, how did you even manage to get out of the country?"

He shrugged. "I told them what they needed to know about the counterfeiters in Macao. That was the price of my freedom. Then they were willing to believe I really didn't have any information about Alan and the Dragon, and only met you by chance." A flicker of his old, rakish grin showed. "I told them how quickly, when we met, you invited me up to your room…"

"I see." She scowled.

"Anyway, losing the reward was expensive, but together we'll turn the Dragon over to the Chinese government and collect an even bigger one."

"Reward!" She spat the word out bitterly, her worst suspicions confirmed. "That's all you think about, isn't it? You and Alan—two of a kind. If all you want is money, why don't you pick up where Alan left off? Why don't you contact the infamous Mr. Yeng?"

"Don't tempt me, C.J.!" His voice was low and threatening, as if she had pushed him too far.

She clamped her mouth shut, deciding it wouldn't be wise to continue the argument. Later, she would make it clear that she was going to Sarawak. They had continued to walk. Despite herself, despite her irritation at him, she was comforted by his nearness.

"Stop," Darius whispered. He pulled her back into the shadows of a doorway, then pointed down the street.

She looked in the direction he was indicating. Through the gray mist, the silhouettes of two men were visible, leaning against the side of a building on the corner, watching the entrance to her hotel. If a taxi pulled up to let out its passengers, they could reach those passengers before they ever got into the hotel.

C.J. knew it was likely that they were waiting for her—wanting to use her to get to Alan and the White Dragon.

"Do you mind leaving a few clothes, if not your heart, in San Francisco?" Darius asked in a hushed voice. "I think we should just get out of here."

She nodded.

He took her arm, and they started to quietly walk back in the direction from which they came. A third man, a hulking figure in a loud plaid sports jacket, stepped directly into their path. He held a gun.

Without even stopping to think about what she was doing, C.J. glanced over the hulk's shoulder. "Alan, no!" she shrieked.

The hulk turned his head for just an instant, but it was enough time for Darius to grab the arm that held the gun.

As the big man tried to shake Darius free, the gun waved wildly. C.J. ran for cover.

"Good thinking, C.J.," Darius said as he twisted the hulk into a wrestling choke hold. The hulk dropped the gun, but then pulled himself free, spun around and flung a fist at Darius. He stepped back quickly, and the blow only landed lightly on his jaw. Retaliation was sweet as his fist smashed into the hulk's face. The man barely staggered before he went after Darius again. Although they were matched in height, the stranger seemed to have a good fifty to sixty pound advantage.

"Don't just stand there, woman. Get the gun!" Darius shouted as he landed another blow to the man's chin, then ducked to avoid the return thrust.

"Stop stepping on it, then!" She couldn't reach the gun for fear of being trampled.

"I'm not—argh!" Darius doubled over as the man hit him in the stomach. He pounded the hulk's rib cage a couple of times in return.

"You do need help!" she said, her hand on her hips.

"Hey, I thought I was doing pretty good. Here!" He gave the gun a kick that sent it spinning along the sidewalk.

C.J. ran for it. "Bravo!" she cried as she swooped down to pick it up. It was huge; it looked more like a hand cannon than a pistol.

She had it in her hand and was about to stop the fight when she saw the two men who had been watching the front of the hotel running toward them. "Uh oh," she murmured.

She looked at the two men approaching from her left, Darius fighting on her right, and had no idea how to stop the men in both directions at the same time. Making her choice, she stood, legs apart in a firm stance, both hands on the handle of the gun, arms straight out in front of her, to face the two runners. It was a position she had seen many times on television, but that was as close as she came to knowing what she was doing.

As soon as they saw the gun, the two men skidded to a stop.

"Stay right there!" she shouted, her voice quaking, the gun shaking violently as she pointed it at them.

"All right, lady," one of the men said, putting his hand up, palm outward. "Just stop shaking. That gun has a hair trigger."

"Be quiet!" she screamed. As she did, the gun jiggled even more.

Seeing that, the two men glanced at each other and nodded then turned and ran as fast as they could away from her and disappeared around the corner. She watched them go with relief, dropping her arms.

Darius! she thought. Spinning around to face the fighters, she raised the magnum again.

The fight had stopped. The hulk was lying on the sidewalk, knocked out cold, and Darius was lounging against the building, one hand in his pocket, the other languidly holding a cigarette to his lips.

She lowered the gun. "Why didn't you help me?" she cried.

"Help you? I thought you were trying out for *Charlie's Angels*. Any minute I expected you to say, 'Come on, make my day!' You did just fine." He laughed as he straightened, then crushed the cigarette on the sidewalk with his toe. "I don't think those guys will stop running until they get to the next county!"

She looked at the gun in her hand and was suddenly filled with loathing. "Let's go!" she said, and tossed it to the ground.

The explosion seemed to rock the entire street. C.J. crouched low and Darius dropped to one knee as a loud hiss filled the air. She looked at the gun barrel, then her gaze followed where it pointed. A gaping hole showed in the tire of a parked car.

C.J. gaped, shocked at what she had done. Darius grabbed her arm and half-dragged her down the block. "Hurry! The police will be here in a minute!"

His words made sense, and she began to run with him.

Three blocks later, she begged him to stop. The pain in her side made it impossible to go any farther. Even the sound of rapidly approaching police sirens couldn't induce her to run another step.

Darius spotted a neighborhood bar, and the two of them walked inside. He ordered them each an Anchor Steam beer, a San Francisco brand, then went to the public telephone.

"We're in luck," he said when he returned to her side. "I contacted the pilot of a small plane who'll take us to Los Angeles International where I can catch a flight to Singapore. You can go home and wait for word from me."

C.J.'s home was a small one bedroom apartment a couple of blocks off busy La Cienega Boulevard. How lonely it suddenly seemed. She didn't care for his suggestion one little bit. "'Go to Jimmy's.' 'Go home.' You are too full of orders, Darius Kane. If Sarawak will be dangerous, it's better for the two of us to stay together."

"Is that it? Or do you think I might run off with the reward money?"

No, Darius, it's not because of money that I can't bear to leave you. But all she said was, "I don't care about the reward. I have to see this through to the end. I'm going to Sarawak, with or without you."

He studied the firm set of her jaw and knew arguing would be useless. "Against my better judgment, I'll agree. Let's have our drinks; the plane will be ready in a couple of hours."

A little while later Darius hailed a taxi for the trip to a small airfield.

By the time they reached Los Angeles International Airport, it was two a.m. They went straight to the ticket counter, C.J. clutching her recently much-abused credit card.

"There's a seven hour wait," Darius said. "That'll give you time to change your mind about going."

"No, but it does allow me to go home and get some clean clothes! I'm sick of wearing the same few outfits."

Darius waited with her at the taxi stand, and as she got into a cab, he got in beside her. She didn't attempt to argue after one look at the expression on his face.

Her apartment was in a 1930's building on a quiet street. The main door was locked, but when she reached her third floor apartment, it was unlocked. Darius had her wait to one side as he went in.

The apartment had been ransacked.

C.J. entered, stunned. "Why?" she whispered, seeing her belongings on the floor, her sofa and overstuffed chair, even her mattress ripped open and the stuffing removed. Her paints were knocked over, and the few paintings she kept in the apartment were thrown in a heap on the floor like so much rubbish.

"Desperation, I guess," Darius said. He glanced at the paintings, and saw what she had said about them—they were purely commercial oils, done quickly and emotionlessly, the sort found lining sidewalks in tourist areas going for around $49 a pop "on sale," and such work was always on sale. He could see she was wasting talent because of a need to make money, a common problem for many people, himself included. No, that wasn't true. His talent was gone now. He turned his thoughts back to the situation at hand. "Whoever did this may have thought Alan sent the White Dragon here, and you or someone close to you might have hidden it. Or, they were sending a message to not even think about trying to hide it here."

"They want me to know they can find me. Scare me." Her gaze was hollow. "Well, they succeeded."

"Find whatever clothes you want to take, C.J., and let's get out of here."

Her shoulders sagged as she stepped over the smashed mementos of her youth and souvenirs from her trip to Europe. She had had so little, and now even that was gone.

Wordlessly, she did as told. Damn that Dragon, anyway, she thought. It would have been better for her and her entire family if it had disappeared with the T'ang dynasty.

They returned to the airport to wait for their flight.

CHAPTER 13

Over twenty-four hours later the plane carrying C.J. and Darius arrived in Singapore. Since there were no flights to the island of Borneo until the next morning, so they had to remain there overnight.

Every muscle in her body was tired and stiff from the long flight, while Darius looked remarkably fresh and rested. Even his day-plus growth of beard served to add to his masculine good looks.

When they stepped out of the air-conditioned airport, the heat and humidity struck like a physical blow. C.J. was surprised at how quickly she forgot about the miserable weather in this part of Asia. She had even looked forward to returning, simply to get away from the disappointments she found at home.

Darius checked his wristwatch. "It's one o'clock. We're going to have to buy some clothes for Sarawak. I suggest we find a hotel first, then shop later. I'm sorry we have to stay here tonight."

"You won't hear any complaint from me. I'm so sick of flying I could scream. My life used to be boring. Now, in the past ten days, I've flown halfway around the world twice. I've been chloroformed, locked in a cellar, involved in one gunfight, two fistfights, had my hotel room and my apartment ransacked, and have nearly been arrested. I didn't know when I was well off!" She frowned.

Darius looked at her in surprise, but then smiled. A smile crept across her face in response.

Darius's smile was nice to see; she had seen far too little of it the last couple of days. She wondered if just being back in Asia had perked up his spirits. Only here did he seem to be completely free of the ghosts of his past. Here, he could forget his disappointments. But how long could he keep running?

In Singapore, just as in San Francisco and Hong Kong, Darius seemed to know his way around.

They found a beautiful hotel on Orchard Road, one of the more modern, luxurious areas of the city. Darius booked two single rooms.

Almost immediately they left the cool comfort of the hotel to do the shopping that would be necessary for their trip into the jungle.

Afterward, Darius wanted to show her the old colonial sector, as well as the area called Kampong Glam, the Muslim part of the city.

As they walked through the city, C.J. discovered that Singapore was lovely. The sun was low, casting a brilliant reddish glow over the skyline, making it appear to shimmer in the heat.

"What do you think," Darius began, "about going back to our rooms, putting on some fresh clothes and going out to dinner?"

"I think," C.J. replied, giving him a sidelong glance, "that sounds wonderful."

Once she reached her room, she was relieved to be alone. She was too aware of him, and all but ached from the strain of repressing any response to him, of keeping far enough away from him that they wouldn't touch, of scarcely allowing her glance to meet his because she knew the longing he might see in her eyes.

Her reaction to him was foolish on her part, well she knew. That route would lead to one thing only, heartache. She'd had enough disappointment for one lifetime; and didn't want any more added to it.

She showered before changing into practical khaki slacks and a white blouse, some of the newly purchased essentials Darius had said she would need in the jungle.

When he stepped into her room, freshly shaven, his hair still damp, wearing a light yellow shirt and white slacks, she gazed at him a little too long. She averted her eyes, but she knew there wasn't much Darius Kane missed.

"Sit on the veranda," she suggested. "Your hair will dry in no time."

"Will you join me?" he asked, rolling back the sleeves of his shirt before stepping into the warm night air.

She nodded.

There was a small table with two chairs. "Would you like me to call room service for drinks?" he asked.

"No thanks." It would be bad enough being alone with him with a clear head; the last thing she needed was liquor.

"C.J.?" he said.

"Yes?"

"Do you have as low an opinion as the British do about my activities in Hong Kong?" His voice was soft, unemotional, but she felt rather than heard the quiet intensity behind his question.

Her brow knitted. Did she? She could understand why he was doing it. He wanted the White Dragon for the reward money, and she was simply a pawn to his ambition. That hurt. "I don't know," she said honestly.

"I see." He fell silent again.

"It's no way to live, Darius. Not for you. You have too much to offer."

He gave a hard, bitter laugh. "I have nothing to offer anyone. No one cares if I'm alive or dead, and that's fine with me."

"Darius!" She looked at him in horror. There was so much she wanted to say. He glanced at her, but she stared at the ground, away from the eyes that missed nothing and questioned everything.

"No big deal, C.J.," he said. "None at all."

He went back indoors.

Had she ever handled anything so badly, she wondered. She remained alone on the veranda, barely able to breathe, the heat oppressive around her. Even though the sun had set, no cooling breezes reached her. She ran her fingers through her hair, pushing it away from her face as she rose then walked back into her room to face Darius.

His back was to her. He sat on the edge of the bed, head bent.

She slid the veranda door shut, then said, "Jimmy Lee told me you believe you aren't good enough to play the piano in public any longer."

He didn't turn, but his back stiffened. "I'm not."

"Maybe you won't be able to perform music so difficult that only you have the skill to perform it, but that doesn't mean you should play nothing."

"When did you become a music critic?" The words dripped with sarcasm.

She wondered if she dare go on, but added, "You still have talent, Darius. I think…I think it eats away at you and that every day you don't use it, a little of you dies inside."

"Oh, so now you're going to psychoanalyze me!" He turned angrily towards her, his eyes flashing, but as their gazes met, he shook his head and remained silent. Her heart ached for him. She didn't really understand obsession, but she knew that the great artists had it —painters, musicians, even the top athletes. They were obsessed with doing the best job they could, with being the best. Nothing less was acceptable. It was what made life meaningful to them. She lacked that fire, just one more bit of evidence that she would never be a great artist, but Darius had it—and it was killing him.

"I'm sorry. That was wrong of me," she said. "There's so much I don't understand about you, much that I simply don't know. I wish it didn't matter to me. I wish you didn't matter, but you do." Minutes seemed to go by as C.J. waited for him to speak.

"You're right," he said finally. "I should tell you; I owe it to you. It may help explain why I live like I do." He paused. "Why I suspect I'll always live this way." The last words were spoken so softly that she barely heard them.

She understood what he was trying to say. She had told herself, time and again, that he was only passing through her life, that eventually she would continue on alone, just as before. That was the practical, logical way to think about this man and all that he meant to her. And she was always practical and logical. Yet, hearing him confirm it hurt more than she imagined.

She crossed the room and sat on a chair, viewing him only in profile.

"I was living in England," he began, his voice unnaturally hollow. "I was married, and believe me, I was on top of the world. Orchestras had started to seek me out to perform with them, and I was negotiating a record contract. The reviews of my performances were more than I could have hoped for.

"I know you've heard of wife, Nadia, generally considered one of the greatest of all Hungarian violinists. We'd met in Paris three years earlier. She was nine years older than me, and her whole life up to that point had been the violin, music and musicians. She was already well-known, though not nearly as famous as she is today. I moved in with her, and when she became pregnant, we got married. She was thirty-six, and wanted a child very badly. I've thought about this a lot over the years, to help myself understand what happened later."

The words had come tumbling out of him in a rush, as if he had to explain as much as he could as quickly as he could, but now he hesitated. C.J. said nothing as she watched the slump of his shoulders, the way his head was bent as he spoke.

"One day—Nadia was about five months pregnant at the time— we decided to go for a drive in the country just outside London. As we drove, a car approached us. I learned later that its tire had blown. Suddenly, it was in our lane, the driver clearly out of control. I turned the wheel to get away from it, but the road was lined with trees. I stepped on the brakes too hard, throwing the car into a skid. I knew we were going to crash. All I could think of was Nadia and the baby, and I reached out, trying to brace her with my arm, to hold her as best I could..."

He stopped again.

"It's lucky you both weren't killed," C.J. said softly.

"Yes. I've been told that many times." His voice was distant, and much quieter when he continued. "I awoke in the hospital, so covered with bandages I looked like a mummy."

C.J. nodded at his attempt at lightness while talking about something so painful to him.

"When the car hit, we both went into the windshield. I had the steering wheel to stop my body, and Nadia, luckily, had my arm to protect her. When we hit, though, the windshield shattered. Fortunately, she had tucked her chin so that her cuts were on her head and not her face; she suffered only a light concussion. The arm and hand I was using to hold her went through the windshield, however, and got sliced up pretty badly in the process. All the cuts were superficial, except one. One shard of glass went through my hand, entering from the palm and coming out the back."

So that was it. C.J. shut her eyes and placed a hand against her chest, feeling a little dizzy. That was the accident Jimmy Lee had referred to. One piece of glass, one fluke accident, had meant so much difference in one man's life.

He continued matter-of-factly. "The doctors were very good. They worked hard to repair all the damage that had been done. A few scars…and a slight loss of sensitivity, a slight numbness in the fingers of one hand, caused by nerve damage. Irreparable nerve damage."

The full effect of his words hit her. "God, Darius, I'm so sorry."

"Yes. Everyone was sorry." He sounded almost bored by his tale. "Especially me. I wouldn't even touch the piano for three years. These days, I've learned to compensate somewhat…. But I can't play like I used to. I'll never be able to play like that again."

"And Nadia?" C.J. asked.

"Nadia liked being married to a rising young pianist. For a while she liked being married to a 'tragic accident,' and she wallowed in the sympathy of well-meaning friends." He sighed. "But she didn't like being married to a bitter has-been. When the sympathy of others stopped, so did her interest. Soon after the baby was born, she began to work again, going on tour and taking the child and a nanny with her. I remained in London, alone. Motherhood suited Nadia well. It was being my wife that bored her. One day she announced she wanted a divorce. She had fallen in love with Othmar Vidyansky."

"Vidyansky—the pianist?"

He gave a harsh chuckle. "That made it especially hard to take. It wasn't a matter of being heartbroken, though; I was quite out of love with her by then. But I was bitter. Very bitter. I left, wanting nothing more to do with Europe, music, any of it."

He looked up briefly then bowed his head again. "That's not altogether true. There was one thing there I didn't want to leave, that it almost killed me to leave. That was my daughter, my Alicia."

He ran his fingers through his hair. "I felt like a failure, C.J. Alicia had her mother, the star, and Vidyansky would be her stepfather. Then there was me, a nobody. I had—I have—nothing to offer her but despair and a life of might-have-beens. So I forced myself to leave her…for her own good."

He fell silent.

"You haven't seen her since?" C.J. asked.

"No. She's better off. I've saved her a lot of disappointment."

C.J. shook her head. He was so mistaken. She thought of her own father and how much she loved him. He had his faults, plenty of them, in fact, but if he weren't there…

Darius looked at her. "What is it?" he asked.

She wasn't sure if she should say anything, but her heart couldn't help but go out to his child. "I can't help but suspect that if your daughter ever got to know you," she said, her voice husky, "she would want you in her life. She would want to see you. You're a fine man, Darius; you have a good heart. I suspect that for your little girl, the accident wouldn't matter. You're her father. She will want to know that you care about her. That you love her."

"You don't make it easy, do you, C.J.?" His pain cut through her.

"I'm sorry," she whispered, bowing her head. She hadn't meant to hurt him; that was the last thing she would ever want to do. But she knew, from the innermost reaches of her being, that he was wrong about his child.

"Please, continue," she said softly. "After you left England, what did you do?"

He shrugged. "I traveled, drank and generally bummed round for almost two years. I ended up in Calcutta, living in a filthy hovel, drunk and miserable. Then, one day, in walked Jimmy Lee. I remember his exact words: 'Darius Kane, it's been over three years since your accident. That's enough self-pity. You're coming home now.' He wouldn't take no for an answer. Home meant Hong Kong. I returned there with him. That was three years ago."

"You're lucky to have such a friend."

He nodded. "I know."

They fell silent as she thought about all he had told her. "So why do the British police think you're a bounty hunter?" she asked.

He shook his head ruefully. "That's such a nasty name for something I don't think is bad. I guess it's true, though. In Hong Kong, especially around Jimmy's friends, I'd hear a lot of things. To me, Hong Kong is the heart of Asia—everyone and everything important passes through it."

"I heard about some Australian bank robbers. They were traced to Jakarta, but the police were stumped. The case interested me, and I got a few leads. I went to Jakarta and discovered the leads were good ones; the robbers were caught, and I received the reward money. The Australian and British police were a little put out by one man showing them up, I guess. As for me, I thought it was pretty easy money. There wasn't much of it, though. I used it to give Jimmy what I felt I owed him. He accepted it; he realized it was a matter of pride."

Expressionless, she nodded and waited.

"From then on, I paid a lot more attention to things I heard. More cases came my way. I've gotten a few big rewards and, with Jimmy's help, made some even bigger investments. The one worthwhile thing I've done was to set up a trust for Alicia. At least she won't think her father took off and left her with nothing. By the tune she's eighteen, she won't need to be dependent on anyone if she doesn't want to be. And that, my dear Corabelle, is the whole sordid tale."

"No, Darius, it's not sordid, just..." She shook her head and bit her bottom lip. She couldn't go on.

He walked to the window, facing the lights of Singapore.

He leaned his hands on the window frame as he began to speak, his back still toward her.

"You know, Cleo, you remind me of the way I saw the world years ago, back when I was young. Before Nadia, before Europe, Asia—when I was just a kid with dreams. There's an innocence about you I thought no longer existed in the world. I'm glad to find it still does."

"Am I really so naïve, Darius?"

"Don't mock it. It's a good thing."

She walked up beside him. "I don't want to be that way. I want..." She drew in her breath and admitted aloud what she'd been holding in heart. "I want to be with you."

He shook his head, a mixture of anger and hurt shadowing his face. "You didn't understand what I was saying!"

"I did understand, more than you know!"

He took hold of her arms. "I'd just be using you. With me, you'd give and give and never receive. In the end, you'd hate it. You'd hate me. I travel around Asia for months on end, tracking down heaven only knows what. Or why. But it's my life now. It's all I've got."

She felt the color drain from her face. "I see," she said, the words barely a whisper, hoping he wouldn't realize that she was crumbling inside. "It's okay, Darius. I never expected anything from you. I simply wanted you to know how I felt." Her words were spoken nonchalantly, as if she hadn't a care in the world.

He dropped his hands without replying.

"Let's go eat now,"—she stood straight, shoulders square, jaw firm, upper lip stiff—"before we both fall into a dead faint from hunger."

She picked up her handbag, opened the door to her room, took a deep breath and was halfway down the hall before Darius caught up to her.

They left the hotel and walked along the sidewalk without speaking.

He confused her. He fascinated her. Everything about him was unique and far beyond her experience. She cherished his vulnerabilities as well as his strengths, his dark moods as well as his humor, his macho bravado as well as his sensitive musical ability. He was a study in contrasts, the most intriguing man she had ever met. But she also saw that he was slowly tearing himself apart, tormented by his own unwillingness to accept life as it was.

And there was nothing she could do about it.

CHAPTER 14

The next day they flew to Kota Kinabalu, to Kuching and then, for a generous fee, found someone to fly them to the jungle clearing called Bir Sakan.

C.J. had wired ahead to Alan's former co-workers that she was coming to pick up his belongings. As the small plane dropped toward the runway, she recognized the man waving in greeting.

"Miss Perkins, how nice to see you again," he said with a Southern drawl so thick she could almost touch it. He held his hand out to help her off the plane.

"Thank you. I hadn't expected anyone to meet us."

"My pleasure." He beamed, giving her hand an affectionate squeeze before he released it. He was a pleasant looking man, tall, with blue eyes, sandy hair and a ruddy, boyish complexion.

Darius stepped out beside her, and she introduced him. "This is Darius Kane, and this is Mister..."

"Hallinan. Hank Hallinan." He held out his hand to Darius. "Pleased to meet you."

"And you," Darius replied as they shook hands.

"I'm sorry," C.J. murmured to Hank, apologizing for forgetting his name.

He smiled warmly at her. "I understand. You were upset when you were here. I felt right bad for you, little lady—"

"By the way," Darius interrupted, putting his hand on C.J.'s shoulder, "I should explain. I'm here to help Miss Perkins. I'm her fiancé."

Hank's eyebrows rose slightly; then he smiled broadly.

"Well, that does explain it, now doesn't it? I was wondering about a sweet young thing like this travelling with some man. But now I see. Why, if she were my intended, I sure wouldn't let her go off to a place like this alone. No sirree, I sure wouldn't." He picked up C.J.'s bag and started back toward his jeep. "Let's get a move on," he called over his shoulder to them.

As soon as Hank's back was turned, C.J. shot Darius a scathing look. "What nerve!" she whispered.

"Nerve? If you can tell strangers I'm your brother, I can certainly tell them you're my 'intended.'" He looked like a kid who'd licked the bowl after making chocolate pudding.

"As if I'd have such bad taste!"

Darius chuckled causing Hank to glance back quickly at the two of them.

They reached the jeep and climbed in for the short ride to the village, C.J. sitting next to Hank, and Darius in the back.

"What's the word on Alan? I reckon you found him," Hank asked.

"Homesickness," C.J. said blandly. "He went to Hong Kong for a while, then just felt he couldn't return here, and went back to the States."

Hank nodded. "Not surprising, I guess. He never did seem content here, always looking over the rainbow. For that pot of gold, you know."

C.J. gave him a quick glance. Did he know something? Or did he simply have more insight into Alan's character than she expected.

"Yes, he's a dreamer," she replied.

They swung into the village. It was just as C.J. remembered it: green and lush, children everywhere, and longhouses on stilts six feet off the ground lining the river. The longhouses could be reached only by ladders, and at night the ladders were pulled inside to protect the families from attack. About fifty families lived in each longhouse, sleeping on mats.

The first time she'd gone to Sarawak, she hadn't known anything about the tribal people, the Iban. This time, on the flight over, she asked Darius to tell her about them.

She soon regretted her curiosity.

The Iban were the original "wild men of Borneo" of P.T. Barnum fame. They had once been headhunters. Heads of their enemies from neighboring tribes would be brought back to the longhouses and placed on shelves. Because the Iban believed a man's spirit continued to live in the head after death, food and cigarettes would be stuffed into the victim's mouth and the cigarettes lit so that the spirit would feel happy.

The government had declared headhunting illegal some years ago and, as far as was officially known or reported, it now happened only about once every five years. But who was counting?

Darius had never been to Sarawak, although he had once traveled to Kalimantan, the Indonesian part of Borneo. In the interior, where the Dayaks, a people similar to but a little less violent than the Iban, lived, he'd seen a number of dried human heads gracing the doorways of the longhouses. To keep the government off their backs, the natives insisted the heads on display had been taken many, many years earlier, but Darius hadn't been so sure about that.

The more C.J. heard, the more nervous she became. Fear of pythons and orangutans paled compared to headhunters.

The two missionaries and Peace Corpsmen whom C.J. had met on her last trip, as well as an unknown white man, were waiting for them when they arrived, along with what looked like the entire village. A stranger's arrival was a rare occurrence that brought everyone out to gawk.

"Alan's in the States," Hank called out as he pulled the jeep to a halt. "He was homesick."

A murmur went through the crowd as everyone commented on the announcement. Hank stood up. "While y'all are here, let me make the introductions. Y'all remember Miss Perkins, I know. This here is her fiancé, Mr. Kane."

Then he turned to C.J. and Darius. "Miss Perkins, you probably remember lots of these folks." He gestured with his hand as he made the introductions. "Here's Zachariah Jenkins and Bill Everett from the Methodist church, Tony Scioza was with Alan and me, and this here is John Carter, Alan's replacement. Kaloo Mangyalubyang is the leader of this village. The mayor, we call him, and his assistant is Malu Butangyang. And all the rest of these here folks will make themselves known to you before the day's out."

Everyone laughed at that and greeted C.J. and Darius warmly.

She felt her skin prickle as the "mayor," Kaloo, took her hand to shake it. He was one of the few Iban who practiced that particular Western custom. Damn Darius's talk of headhunters, she thought. Kaloo was dressed in his finest clothes: red batik material around his hips with a silver belt holding a white loincloth and the batik in place. On his head was a magnificent headdress of bright multicolored material, shaped like a ten-inch hatbox, and topped with six long, rather ugly gray feathers. His skin was light brown with complex black tattoos covering both arms. When he smiled in greeting, C.J. saw that more teeth were missing than not.

She and Darius were led by Hank toward the "short" version of a longhouse, where the foreigners lived. "That room there," he said to C.J., pointing at a door in the long building, "was Alan's place. It's John's now, but so that you can have it while you're here, he's sharing my room."

C.J. faced John Carter. "Thank you, that's very kind," she said with a smile, but was surprised to see a frown on his face. He smiled back as soon as he realized she was looking at him, but there was no sincerity in his gaze.

"Mr. Kane can, uh, bunk with Tony," Hank sputtered. C.J. smiled inwardly at his obvious discomfort at not knowing just how to deal with this relationship. Unmarried couples often shared rooms in the U.S., but in Sarawak? And right under the noses of two missionaries? It wasn't going to happen.

"Fine," Darius said, also recognizing the man's quandary.

The full coterie of men walked C.J. to the ladder that led to "her" room.

She climbed up and entered the tiny room alone. It hadn't changed much since the last time she'd been there. A wafer-thin mattress lay on one of the few solid spots in the floor. Elsewhere, there were missing slats and warped pieces that protruded higher than the rest. One hole in the floor was there on purpose. It provided the Iban-style bathroom facility. Bamboo mats to sit on, shelves, a kerosene lamp and a small chest of drawers made up the rest of the furniture.

"Miss Perkins?" a male voice called to her from outside.

"Come in, please."

John Carter entered the room. He was of average height, with a stocky build. He had brown hair, thinning at the crown, yet he looked fairly young, in his mid-twenties, C.J. guessed. His features were plain, making him the type of man one wouldn't bother to notice in a crowd. He wore jeans and a T-shirt—the standard foreigner dress in Sarawak.

"I hope I'm not disturbing you," he said, his dark brown eyes studying her.

"Not at all."

"I tried to leave everything as your brother had it, in case he came back."

"I see. You didn't believe this assignment would be permanent, then?"

"I didn't know. It was all so unexpected." He smiled. "Alan's in the U.S., you said?"

"Yes."

"Back home?"

"No." Was he just being polite, or was there a purpose to this?

"It must have been a pleasant surprise for you to find him so easily." Again, the ingratiating smile was flashed at her.

C.J. was thankful for her artistic training, guessing that was what made her so aware that the look in his eyes was at odds with the smile on his lips. "Actually, I didn't find him. He contacted my parents and told them he was fine. That's all," she lied.

"I see. How nice for you. I...we were all surprised that you would come to pick up his belongings personally. We could have packed them up and shipped them. The expense of this visit must be tremendous."

She and Darius had wondered who would ask that question first, and they had figured out their response. "Darius once lived in Kota Kinabalu in Sabah. He wanted to see it again, and I wanted to see it for the first time. This was a good excuse for us to come to Borneo."

"You must be wealthy."

How rude of him, she thought, to persist with these questions.

"Not me." She gave him a telling look, hoping to embarrass him into silence.

But he continued. "So Alan will soon be back in Columbus, Ohio, and his sister is sightseeing. A happy ending for the family."

He knew about Columbus. The others must have told him. "No. He'll never go back to Columbus. Nothing is there for him." Something about this man's questions was bothering her, and she felt the need to steer any possible interest away from her parents' home. "I think he's going to live in New York City." It was one place she knew he'd never move to.

"Well, it's almost suppertime. They've prepared a bit of a feast to celebrate your arrival. They couldn't party during your last visit because of the circumstances, so the village wants to make it up to you this time."

"How nice!" C.J. was both surprised and warmed by such thoughtfulness.

A short while later she went outdoors with Carter. Hot as her room had been, it seemed cool in comparison to the outdoors. The heat was intense, but the humidity was even worse. The air was so filled with moisture she couldn't believe it wasn't raining.

Darius and the others joined them. True to John Carter's word, the village had prepared a huge meal of hot, spicy and unrecognizable meat, fish, and fowl; rice; and leafy unfamiliar vegetables. The meat had a musty pungency to it that not even spices could cover. Much as she tried, C.J. couldn't put out of her mind the many rat-like animals that dwelled under the longhouses and lived off the refuse and garbage. They could easily have become part of the meal now gracing the dinner table. Being a guest, she managed to swallow enough to hopefully avoid insulting her hosts.

The local liquor flowed freely, while the villagers performed music and dancing. Screaming dancers wearing feathers and animal skins wheeled and soared in mock battles. A young man danced with a traditional *mandau*, the wide sword of the headhunter. He whirled the sword and leaped about to wild gamelan music. C.J. didn't want to admit that her hair stood on end as she watched him, and she drank more than she should have while that performance was going on. Less aggressive dances followed.

The evening was long, but fascinating.

She put all thoughts of John Carter and his questions out of her mind until Darius walked her to her room and said good-night. "Wait," she whispered. "I need to talk to you."

As he followed her up the ladder, she could feel the knowing glances and smiles of the villagers.

Ignoring them, she relayed her conversation with Carter and her concern over his questions.

"You were right not to tell him—or anyone else—anything that can lead to Alan," he said.

"Something else bothers me. Why would the Peace Corps replace Alan so soon? I've never known the government to do anything quickly. How would they know he wasn't coming back? Do they have ties to the police? It doesn't make sense."

He looked away from her, as if not wanting her to read the same questions in his eyes. Or did he have the answers?

"I'm sure there's a simple explanation," he said off-handedly. "It's probably nothing. I'll see you in the morning."

As he turned to leave the hut, C.J. whispered good-night, her eyes following him. He glanced over his shoulder at her before stepping outside, while she stood as if rooted to the spot.

She watched a look of uncertainty cross his face. Although he had made it quite clear that they had no future, she wondered if it was in some way almost as hard for him to leave her as it was for her to watch him go.

She was thankful when her old sense of humor returned and she smiled.

"What is it?" he asked.

"Well, I was just thinking, I always pictured you in a little grass shack, with wild, primitive nature at your feet, and here you are. I'm glad I got to see you here. The picture is perfect."

His gaze burned as he looked at her. Then he left without another word.

CHAPTER 15

The next morning C.J. arose and went in search of Darius only to learn that he had already gone into the jungle alone. She hurried back to her room. Her notebook with the map Alan had drawn was gone.

She felt both perplexed and angry. Would Darius try to find the White Dragon without her? Would he take it out of Sarawak to get the reward? Or would he sell the jade to Yeng for even more money? And if he found it, would he come back to see her one last time?

She wandered around the village for the rest of the morning, growing more irritated at Darius's absence by the minute. Finally she went into one of the longhouses, where she tried to help the women husking rice. She was sure they tolerated her only out of hospitality. About noon, she saw Darius casually strolling back into the village, hands in his pockets, whistling a jaunty tune. She hurried outside to wait, arms folded and foot tapping.

"What did you think you were doing?" she asked as soon as he was within hearing distance. "I thought we were going out there together!"

"Just checking the territory. I decided it would be best not to take you into something that could be dangerous before looking at it first-hand. Borneo does have cobras and leopards, even rhinoceros. Most of them don't live in this swampy coastal area, luckily. But there's enough that is lethal here that I was worried."

She was tired of being treated like a helpless child. "I know Alan wouldn't go anywhere dangerous!"

"As I've said before, Alan lived here for three years. He learned what to watch out for."

"Well then," she asked, glaring, "what now?"

"Lunch." He walked off, leaving her standing there gawking at him. Finally she followed.

Their lunch of fresh fruit, rice and tea made her feel a bit more human—enough so that when Darius said he was going to take a walk along the beach, she decided to go with him.

The ocean was about two mile from the river village, at the end of a well-worn trail. A slight breeze blowing in off the water helped her to feel more comfortable than she had since her arrival.

Darius seemed to be spending far more time watching her than the scenery. Finally it began to upset her. "Is anything wrong?" she asked.

He shook his head and glanced at her again, then looked out at the ocean. Dark clouds filled the sky directly overhead.

"C.J., I…" He hesitated, then began to walk along the sandy beach again in silence.

She followed, her frustration growing. "What is it?"

"Nothing. Let's go back."

"Right," she snapped. "Let's go back." She stuffed her hands in her pockets as they retraced their steps. Everything about him that day had infuriated her—the way he had taken Alan's map and gone exploring without her, the way he kept trying to frighten her about the jungle, the way he seemed to be keeping something from her, and particularly the way he was avoiding any conversation. "Obviously we have nothing to say to each other," she added with more than a hint of petulance.

He didn't even bother to pretend she was wrong.

A strong wind gusted in from the ocean.

"If the rain starts," he said quietly, looking at the sky, "we had better wait here. A beach is safer than the jungle in a tropical storm."

She put her hands on her hips. "In that case I'll just have to make it back before the rain ever starts, because I wouldn't wait out a storm with you in Buckingham Palace, let alone on this beach."

She saw his anger flare as quickly as hers had as she marched into the jungle.

When a few large drops of rain started to fall, C.J. began running toward the village. She hadn't gotten very far when the rain picked up. Never had she been in such a torrential downpour. She was soaked in no time. Strangely, in the jungle, even the rain felt hot and steaming.

The trees started swaying wildly, and vines began to fall.

As the storm strengthened, the jungle turned gray from the sheeting water, and she could barely see where she was going. The wind, rushing through the leaves, was deafening. She stopped and looked at the trees in alarm, as the sound of cracking wood and crashing timber was heard nearby. In a matter of minutes the jungle had become frightening, menacing. She pushed her wet hair off her face and stumbled ahead.

"You little fool!" Darius caught her arm, stopping her progress. He was as soaked as she was, his clothing clinging to him.

"Let's hurry!" She jerked her arm free and took a step away from him.

"You don't know what you're doing." He grabbed her, spun her around to face him. Her hair slapped against her face, and he brushed it back roughly before his hands clasped her shoulders. "These rain-storms don't last long, but they can be dangerous. They turn the ground into a river full of poisonous snakes and lizards. The trees droop, blocking the trails; vines and branches fall—and who knows what kind of creatures will come hurtling down with them?"

She stared at him in disbelief.

"Look at the ground," he said.

She looked down. Already the water was eddying around her ankles. At the thought of snakes in it, she blanched.

Darius put his arm around her. "Come on," he said. She wasn't about to argue. The sooner he got her out of there, the better. She held on to his waist, her fingers clutching his shirt as the water and mud beneath her feet grabbed at her boots, making walking difficult.

"Over there," he shouted as the storm kicked itself into a fury. He pointed to a raised, rocky area. Slowly they made their way to it, scrambling up the hard granite until they reached a smooth flat area that abutted a cliff face with a hollowed out area offering protection from the rain.

"What a mess!" C.J. couldn't help but laugh. She was completely soaked, and pushed her hair off her face. "I've never seen anything like it! It's wild, but strangely beautiful. Come back here with me. It's a little dry, at least." She held out her hand to Darius, and he took it as he stepped closer, huddled under the granite.

Her hand tightened on his and she lifted her gaze to him. Their eyes met and everything seemed to stop.

Without thought, she opened her arms, and he stepped into them, then wrapped her in his grasp. His mouth found hers before she had a moment to think about it, to protest, or to walk away. She felt his muscles harden beneath her hands as the intensity of the kiss sparked and grew.

Her eyes caught Darius's, and the look on his face was one of smoldering hunger, a naked desire that shocked her, causing her breath to catch, a hunger matched by her own. Her hands, her traitorous hands, opened wide and glided over his back, pressing him hard against her. She exulted in the taste of him, the feel of him. Everything about him was strong and forceful. His heartbeat could have been hers, so closely were they bonded.

Something about this wild place, the jungle, the pelting, savage rain, merged with the feel of him, her dangerous jungle man, to unleash the desire she had been struggling against. She wanted him completely. It was always there, this powerful ache, but she had denied and suppressed it for so many days and nights that now, awakened, there was no holding back. She was sure her feelings were apparent to him, and she had no ability or wish to hide them.

He raised his head, his eyes fixed on hers, then to her mouth. "I must be a real bastard, Cleo," he whispered, a tortured look on his face. "Despite my honorable intentions, you make me want things that are wrong—wrong for you."

His words cut through her. She saw the unhappiness in his face, heard the desperation in his voice, and, as always, though she knew it would only lead to more heartache, she saw beneath the surface dismissal of his words to the man who needed the love she felt for him, whether he could admit it or not.

Her fingers trembled as she slid them over his face, his chin, his lips. "I love you," she whispered, her voice husky and her eyes like gray smoke.

His face filled with an anguish that she felt reflected in her own as time passed and she realized that he couldn't respond in kind to the words she had spoken. Despair crept through her for her foolish, revealing words.

"C.J.," he whispered, cupping her face. "Don't look at me like that. Don't—" He kissed her softly, desperately, and then once more.

Her body trembled beneath his touch, aching for his caresses. Dazed, she watched the play of emotions running over his face. Then, with boldness she didn't know she possessed, she lowered herself to the ground, took his hand, and drew him down beside her. Hungrily, his kisses deepened as his hands slid over her body.

His touch was like a blazing bonfire in the midst of the storm, a haven in the oceans of water swirling and beating down upon them. She no longer cared about the water, the noise, the crawling, slithering creatures, any of it. They were nothing to her, not even as clothes were shed and used as a cushion beneath them. They were nothing compared to the fire that Darius caused to burn in her very being, the fire that totally consumed her.

She lost track of everything as a pulsating ache filled her and she kissed him desperately, whispering his name over and over, knowing on some instinctual level that only he had the power to help her now. Yet, despite the fever that filled her, she couldn't stop herself from stiffening as their passion neared its inevitable conclusion. It's Darius, she told herself. Darius, with his fluid grace and rakish features, his tender kindness and watchful concern. Darius, who had never hurt her, who had been there when she needed him. Darius, the man she had fallen head over heels in love with, the man she wanted to be her first lover, her only lover.

Holding him tightly, she pushed hard against him.

He stopped. He didn't make a move or say a word, but as he stayed frozen above her, she knew he realized the full extent of her deception. Much as she'd tried, she hadn't been able to fool him.

Her head was spinning, her heart beating so loudly that she could hear it drumming wildly in her ears even over the loud rush of the storm. A long moment passed before he seemed to expel the breath he had been holding. She thought she heard him whisper her name, thought she heard him say, "Oh, C.J.," but she wasn't sure. Perhaps it was just a groan…

Perhaps she was no good at this, and that was why he had stopped. Perhaps she was unable to give him any pleasure at all and never should have decided to try. Perhaps he would despise her now....She fought the tears that welled up in her eyes.

Slowly, with infinite tenderness, his mouth found hers. His fingers lightly touched her face, as if he could tell where the rain stopped and her tears began. Gently, he kissed the tears away, and it struck her as so wonderful a gesture that it was all she could do to prevent more tears from falling.

She put her arms around him, looking at the outline of his face, his beautiful face, as the wonder filled her of how intimately their bodies had joined, of how perfectly they were made for each other. A warmth spread through her, and she was sure it radiated from her whole body.

He waited, as if understanding every nuance of her feelings. When his lips found hers, the fire in the kiss kindled and grew. There was no more she could want, no more she could hope for. He made love to her with perfect gentleness, until she was lost in another world, another plane. Then, together, they slowly floated back down to earth.

Darius didn't move for a long time. Finally, he propped himself up on his elbows, leaned forward and kissed her. "Are you all right?" he asked.

"All right?" She turned her head away from him, wondering what he must be thinking. A woman of her age...

He moved to her side then, his arms still around her, his body still pressed against hers.

"Of course, I'm all right," she said. Then, her heart heavy, she asked the question that was torturing her. "Are you sorry for having anything to do with me? Someone with no experience, no—"

"Stop, C.J." He lightly kissed her as if in quiet dismay at her pain. "I'm not sorry, never that. But you could have told me."

"I wasn't totally ignorant was I? I've read books, seen movies. I know I'm plain but—"

"Plain?! You're the least plain woman I've ever known. You're beautiful, in body and soul."

If he kept saying such nice words to her, he was going to make her cry again. And hadn't she already revealed enough of herself to him? She sat up. "I'm getting pretty old, you see." She spoke quickly, force-fully as she quickly pulled on her wet clothes. "And I did want to experience…You're not without some physical attraction. Just think of it as research. To help my artwork."

He was standing, jeans on, trying to untwist his wet pullover, when her words hit. "Research? Is that all it was? Really?"

His question surprised her. Not only had he not laughed at her inexperience, but he seemed genuinely to care about her. "Perhaps… there was more. A bit."

He said nothing for a long time, and slowly, she felt his tension ease. "C.J. Perkins, you are such a sham. Someday maybe you'll learn to trust me."

And then, as quickly as it began, the storm ended. The village lay not far away.

CHAPTER 16

*O*nce they were back in the village, C.J. told the Peace Corpsmen that they planned to go out the next day to take some pictures. That was the usual pastime for visitors, and since Darius was obviously a man who knew how to take care of himself, no objections were raised. Some native women offered to fill their knapsacks with provisions for the next day's trek as soon as they finished packing food for some villagers who were going hunting for a few days.

Back in C.J.'s room, Darius removed her notebook from his hip pocket. Before he gave it back to her, he tore out Alan's map, blotted it dry as best he could and put it in his own pocket. She saw, but didn't say anything. Too much had already been left unsaid between them.

"I should go," Darius said. "I'm sure the missionaries are watching the door to room."

She nodded, her heart beating hard and fast. "I'm sure."

He looked at her a long moment without moving, then walked to the door. "Will you paint this, C.J.?" His voice was choked, husky. "Will you paint Sarawak for me?"

She wanted to go to him then, wanted to hold him again, to find out if making love could be as magical the second time as it had been the first. But something held her back. "Of course," she whispered. She would never forget being here with him.

"Promise?"

What's wrong? She wanted to cry out, but only said, "Yes."

He nodded and left.

Darius was back before the sun was up. "Get dressed, we've got to get going."

"Why so early?" she mumbled, turning over to go to sleep again.

"The fewer people who see us, the less likely we are to be followed."

They put on khakis, heavy boots and helmet-like safari hats, then set out, entering the jungle with caution. She struggled not to scream every time she saw some huge, unnamable creature slither by. Soon they left the path the villagers had made. The jungle closed in around them. It held an amazing amount of life: birds, lizards and bugs of all shapes, sizes and colors. Most of the larger jungle animals were nocturnal, for which C.J. was grateful. In the distance, she heard cries and caws—a constant hum—from the jungle's denizens, but where they walked the noise stopped, as if every living creature sensed the strangers in their midst and stayed still until they passed.

Darius pointed out landmarks along the way. He made it very clear that she was to pay close attention to every little detail, because if anything were to happen to him, she would have to make it back alone. The thought made her shudder, but she nodded, and hoped he didn't see how terrified the notion made her.

"Keep away from those," he said, pointing off in the distance.

Her eye followed his finger's direction and she saw, under a large fern, an enormous lizard. She grimaced. "I wouldn't dream of going near one."

"They're poisonous."

"I didn't need to know that."

A short while later he held out his arm. "Stop," he said.

"Let's go this way." He took her arm to lead her around the area they had been approaching.

"Why?" she asked. All she saw was a tree ahead of them, just another tree. And they were already completely surrounded by trees, so what was the difference? Then she looked up. The limbs of the tree seemed to be moving. She stopped walking, fascinated, and peered closer as Darius tried to lead her away.

"Baby pythons," he said.

"Oh, my God!" she cried as the slithering, pulsating tree limbs suddenly made sense to her. Little snakes were swarming everywhere. Her blood turned to ice, and her stomach rolled over. All she wanted was to run, but Darius held her firmly by his side.

"It's okay. No need to run," he advised.

She gripped his hand tightly and walked along, her legs shaking, trying to still the pounding of her heart, realizing now that she not only had to worry about what was at her feet, but also what was lurking overhead. For the first time, the heavy hat she wore made sense to her. She knew there were pythons in Sarawak, as well as cobras, but she had irrationally hoped they weren't in this part of the jungle. No such luck. She felt cold beads of perspiration on her brow.

They walked on for another hour, since the morning was still young and relatively cool, until they came to an open area with a few boulders. "Are you hungry?" he asked.

"Starved."

"Let's have breakfast here." He poured coffee from the thermos, then brought out the beef jerky the missionaries had provided, and rice balls and dried-fish from the Malays.

"I'll pass on the fish," C.J. said.

"Do you still know the way back?" he asked.

"Of course."

"Where?"

She looked around then consulted the compass Darius insisted she not only carry but also use. "That way," she said, pointing. "Straight south until you come to the stream. Then you cross it, walk up—no, downstream until you find a slight clearing, find the tallest mountain in the distance and walk in the exact opposite direction, in other words east, until you find the high embankment with three large boulders, turn, hmm, left, and keep going. Eventually you'll find the village—or at least the sea, and from there you can find the village. But I don't know why you're so insistent. I wouldn't dream of going anywhere without you, believe me!"

"The jungle can turn into your enemy in the twinkling of an eye. You always have to know the way out, an exit strategy. I call it the 'backdoor,' and when I enter something new, strange and potentially dangerous, I always try to figure out the backdoor first. Remember that, C.J. It will do you good in life."

They were finishing the meal when they heard a terrible crashing noise. C.J. nearly jumped out of her skin.

The world stood still as she looked around.

Darius grabbed her hand and began to run across the open area toward the trees. A man leaped in front of them with an unearthly cry. His skin was the color of wet earth, and he wore only a loincloth, tooth-laden necklace, and black sooty designs across his face and chest. His spear seemed at least eight feet tall.

C.J. screamed and stopped running, but Darius didn't. His grip tightened as he pulled her after him into the trees and then kept going. She had never moved so fast, and all but flew through the jungle. He pointed towards a massive boulder, and they ran towards it.

Darius flung her behind it, raised his shotgun and fired. She sat, huddling on the ground beside the granite, trying to catch her breath and listening to the pounding of what sounded like hundreds of feet crashing through the jungle after them.

Tears stung her eyes. Could they be headhunters? They're not supposed to be here, not this close to civilization.

Darius fired again, and the noise of running stopped. The jungle became absolutely quiet.

"Let's go," she whispered, desperate, barely able to get the words out of her mouth.

"You go. I'll hold them off."

She couldn't believe what she'd heard and swallowed hard. "No! Please, let's run, before they come back." She grabbed his sleeve, wanting to pull him after her.

"They haven't gone." He crouched behind the rock, looking at her intently. "They're still there, waiting. We can't outrun them, and if they circle us, that's it. Our only hope is for me to keep them here while you get away and bring help."

"But..." Tears did come this time, and she looked at him blankly, helplessly.

"Go!" he ordered. "Now."

She shook her head. "I can't!"

They heard the rustling of leaves. The headhunters were coming closer.

He stood, peering over the rock. "You've got to, Cleo! We have no choice."

She was petrified. It was a joke, she thought. The Peace Corpsmen were having fun—or the villagers. It was a joke, or a nightmare. *Please, God, let me wake up.*

Then she heard more movement, closer this time.

Quickly, he kissed her. "Trust me, C.J. I'll be all right. Just trust me."

Stunned, she nodded.

"When I shoot, you run," he whispered. "Do you understand?"

"Yes."

"Go!" he shouted, then began firing his rifle.

Somehow her legs moved. As if in a dream she plunged deeper into the jungle. The noises behind her told her that the headhunters were still there. The jungle closed between her and Darius. She was alone.

At first she ran crouched over, her legs wobbly as she hurried through the deep brush. After a while, she stood upright and let her feet fly over the rocks, snakes, nests—all these things she had so gingerly skirted before. Her only thought was to get help, to help Darius. She knew nothing about the people who had attacked them, who or what they were, and not knowing her enemy made them that much more frightening.

She thanked God that Darius had made sure she paid close attention to their route. It would have been easy to simply let him guide her, to pay no attention. But if she had, she would have been no help to him at all. She would have been lost herself, floundering until nightfall, when her misery would have been ended in any one of a number of truly horrible ways.

She didn't think about the pain in her side that caused her to nearly double over, or that her lungs felt ready to burst, or that her legs hurt so badly that she could hardly move them. She concentrated on the words she'd heard in interviews after marathons in the U.S.— that you can run through the pain. Don't give in, keep on going and eventually the pain is gone. You can put it past you; you can rise above it.

Her pace slowed, but she didn't stop no matter how high the heat and humidity grew, or how loudly her body begged her to stop. Then, somehow, the pain did stop, and she continued on. Pretend you're not here, her mind told her.

Pretend Darius is safe, and so are you. Pretend you're together again, back in Hong Kong, high atop Victoria Peak.

There were no dangers, no worries. Only her and Darius. No more thoughts of Alan...Alan...

The pain came back; this time she had to stop. She dropped to her knees and held her stomach, bending over, her head nearly touching the ground. Perspiration dripped from her body in rivers. I'm almost there, she thought. Just a little farther.

She rose and stumbled forward, forcing her legs to move despite the pain, despite the perspiration in her eyes blinding her. .

Suddenly hands grabbed her from behind. She screamed and spun toward the headhunter, only to come face to face with one of the villagers from Bir Sakan.

"Darius," she cried, scarcely recognizing the raspy sound of her voice. "We have to help him. Get help. Guns. Quickly, please. Quickly."

The man ran off, and she sank to the ground, vomiting from pain, worry and fatigue. She rolled onto her back, trying to restore some strength. She needed to lead the party back to Darius.

Darius could protect himself; he could take care of himself. If there was anyone on earth who would be able to hold off that attack, it was Darius. Or so she tried to tell herself.

"Miss Perkins?"

She opened her eyes. Hank, John Carter, Kaloo and a number of other villagers were standing over her. Hank quickly knelt by her side and stroked her forehead. "Here, drink this." He lifted a canteen to her lips.

She took it, then pulled herself to her feet. She looked at the men, and then at the guns in their hands.

"Follow me." She began running toward the jungle, but Hank grabbed her arm and stopped her.

"What happened?"

"Men. Natives. Headhunters. I don't know! They attacked us. They had spears. There were hundreds of them. Darius is back there. Please, let me show you. Hurry!"

The men gave each other looks of surprise and skepticism. Finally Hank spoke. "Okay, Miss Perkins. Don't worry, we'll find him. You lead the way." His voice was calm and comforting.

Somehow she forced herself to run again, afraid that too much time had already passed. She hated her inability to run faster, she hated her weakness, the way her own body betrayed her when she needed it most, when she needed it to help her protect the one person who meant the world to her.

It seemed an eternity before they reached the area where she and Darius had lunch, their backpacks and thermos lying on the ground. She collapsed on the backpack, pointing in the direction the others had to go. Hank stayed with her as the others continued forward.

She lay on the ground, bathed in her own perspiration, her limbs trembling uncontrollably from the agony her muscles had endured. She buried her face in her arms.

It was too quiet. The thought screamed at her. Too quiet! Where was everyone? She struggled to her feet, her legs so rubbery they could scarcely hold her. "Darius? We've got to help him. Where is he?"

"Whoa there, little lady." Hank captured her by the waist and held her back as she tried to hurl herself in the direction the men had gone. "They'll find your boyfriend. You sit tight now, you hear?"

Her legs buckled, and she fell to the ground again. They waited for a half hour, forty-five minutes, an hour. She couldn't bear it any longer and began to get up, but her muscles had stiffened so badly that she barely could stand.

"They can't find him, Hank," she said, her voice tiny and scared; it sounded to her like that of a child. "I've got to help. I'll find him."

"Now, why don't we wait here? It'll be okay, I'm sure."

"I can't. He needs me." She brought her hands to her cheeks. "I can't just sit here. God, where is he?"

"He's all right, I'm sure. We haven't had any trouble around here in a few years." Hank's voice was comforting; it made C.J. want to believe whatever he told her. "We'll go, but slowly."

He took her arm, and they walked toward the spot where she had left Darius. They found the boulder where she had last seen him, but there was no sign of him. She had no idea which way to turn.

"Maybe he got away and doubled back toward the village," Hank suggested. "He might be there right now, sitting and waiting for us."

"Do you think so?" she asked with hope.

"Why sure. Since he had a gun and they didn't, the odds are on his side. I know he's okay. That's a man who can take care of himself."

C.J. smiled at him, filled with gratitude for his encouragement.

They walked deeper into the jungle. Soon, they heard the other men talking and heading their way.

C.J. stopped. Hank took her arm.

Then they appeared: John, Kaloo and the other villagers. That was all. Her eyes went to Kaloo, to the rifle he carried. The blood drained from her face. It was Darius's.

She looked at the men, but they turned away. They couldn't meet her eyes.

She stared at the gun. "Where is he?" she whispered.

"We couldn't find him," Kaloo replied.

Hank held her as if afraid she might faint. But she wasn't that weak. "I'll find him!" she said, taking a step.

Hank's hold on her arm tightened, and he held her back. "We'll send a search party out."

"Let go of me!" She yanked her arm free and stumbled away from him. She nearly fell; her body drained. She took another step and stopped, swaying, unable to force herself onward. This isn't real, she thought. It isn't happening.

"I couldn't get here in time," she cried. "I failed him. After all he did to help me, I failed." Tears fell down her cheeks as a searing pain tore through her heart. She threw her head back and looked heavenward. Her eyes caught the green leaves of the treetops in the light of the sun.

They were forcing her away, forcing her back toward the village. "Please stop," she whispered. "We can't go back to the village. There may still be time. We've got to find him."

"John and Kaloo and some others are out there searching. It's growing late. If they have no luck, tomorrow we'll put together a big search party. We'll find him. I promise, Miss Perkins," Hank said gently.

She moved along mutely, Hank and Tony each holding one of her arms. There was nothing left to say.

Back at the mission, Zachariah, who had had some medical training, gave her a powerful tranquilizer, and she sank into oblivion.

CHAPTER 17

She awakened to a small candle lighting the room. She looked around, trying to think through the heavy fog that enveloped her brain. She felt alone, more alone than ever before in her life, consumed by a terrible, all-encompassing emptiness. Then she remembered that there was someone, a place of shelter. She struggled to reach him, but something, someone, held holding her back, refused to allow her to go on.

"Darius!" she murmured. He would come to her; he would save her, just as he had so many times in the past. She would never have to worry again; she would always be safe with him. "Darius!" The name became a sob.

In the foggy haze her world had become, she felt someone holding her down, softly speaking words she didn't understand, forcing a bitter liquid down her throat. She coughed and sputtered. Then all went black, and the pain stopped.

The next time she opened her eyes, sunlight was shining through the doorway of the bungalow.

Hank stood beside her. "Hello, there," he said, his voice soft and gentle.

"Hank," she whispered. She tried to sit up, only to find her whole body throbbed painfully. Then she remembered, and her eyes shut again. She was too frightened to ask what she needed to know. Too frightened of what the answer might be. Instead, she whispered, "What time is it?"

"Seven o'clock…in the morning. We gave you some medicine to help you sleep."

She let the words sink in. He said nothing about Darius. If the news was good, he would have told her. She knew without asking, but couldn't stop herself. "Did…"

"No." It was more like a groan than a word.

She shut her eyes, and, silently, her tears fell.

They brought her food. Broth was the only nourishment she could get past her lips. She didn't want to move, to eat, to face reality.

The next morning the sun was bright. She dressed and left the longhouse. Her eyes were so swollen and sore from tears they could barely function. Then she saw the jungle, an ever-present, living, fearful entity.

She walked away from the longhouses. She had no tears left to shed. Why had it happened? She asked that question over and over. Why?

The large search party Hank had gathered returned the previous night. They had found no sign of Darius, but there was a rumor in some of the northern villages that a white man had been killed. Hank assured C.J. that it was just a rumor.

She stayed three more days. Another search party went out, but returned with no more luck than the first.

She despised Bir Sakan and everything about it. At the same time, she had memories of two days there with Darius that she would treasure the rest of her life. The people were kind, casting her glances filled with pity. But she didn't want their friendship or their pity. There was only one person whose company she wanted, and this place had taken him from her.

John Carter was the only one who didn't offer her pity. His eyes were always on her, watching her every move. She didn't care, and usually ignored him.

One afternoon he walked up beside her as she sat alone in the sun, sipping a cool drink and watching some children playing a few feet away. "It's a pretty good gig, C.J."

She looked up at him, shielding her eyes with her arm, not having any idea what he was talking about.

"You and your friend," he continued. "Clever. They told me you were."

What was he talking about? Her clever friend. Darius, The familiar desolation swept over her. "Yes, Darius was clever. Clever and wonderful. John, I..." She stopped, her voice deserting her, and leaned back in her chair, then turned silently to face the jungle.

He gave her a curious look, then rubbed his chin and walked away. He said nothing more to her.

On the fifth day after Darius's disappearance, a charter plane flew into Bir Sakan to pick her up. She had already packed up Alan's few belongings into two cardboard boxes and mailed them to her parents' house. She also packed Darius' and her suitcases. Remembering their time in Singapore, buying the clothes to take with them, made the packing of them one of the hardest things she ever had to do.

Much to her surprise, John Carter insisted on accompanying her to Kuching. He said she was in no condition to travel alone. Hank had radioed information about Darius's disappearance to the Sarawak government, and a formal statement had to be filed. Carter offered to make the statement and answer any official questions.

The charter flight took them to Kuching, where it took over three hours for C.J. and Carter to pass on about fifteen minutes' worth of information. She was exhausted and miserable when the ordeal ended.

Rather than remain overnight in Sarawak waiting for the next afternoon's Malaysian Airline System flight to Kota Kinabalu in Sabah, Carter hired another charter for that afternoon.

Again, he insisted on accompanying her. She could understand him wanting to clear up Darius's disappearance with the Sarawak government, but his decision to go all the way to the province of Sabah was too much. She neither needed nor wanted his company. A fleeting thought that he was following her flickered through her mind, but then was lost, leaving only a small residue of annoyance at his nearness.

In Kota Kinabalu she learned that there would be a flight to Hong Kong the next afternoon. Carter got them adjacent rooms in a small hotel and took her to dinner.

She hardly tasted her meal; all she wanted was to go back to her room and be left alone. The next morning he escorted her to a late breakfast and then the airport.

Not until she was on the plane to Hong Kong, finally out of his view, did she fully realize how stifling he had been, how closely he had inspected her every word and gesture. She was glad to be alone.

From the plane, she gazed down at the South China Sea, glad she had decided to fly directly to Hong Kong from Sabah. She hadn't had the heart to take the more popular route, through Singapore.

She never wanted to see Singapore again. She didn't want to do anything but go home and forget all about Asia. She hated it here. But she couldn't go home quite yet. There was one more stop she had to make. She had to see Jimmy Lee and tell him, in person, what had happened.

She owed that much to him—and to Darius.

Her heart skipped a beat as she caught her first glimpse of Hong Kong. It was beautiful, alive. It seemed Darius should be down there somewhere.

She caught a taxi outside the airport and gave the driver Jimmy's address on the Peak. She hadn't even thought about going to a hotel first, only that she needed to see Jimmy. Slowly, the taxi fought its way through the traffic of Kowloon, then through the Cross Harbour Tunnel to Hong Kong Island. C.J. realized why Darius had preferred to take the tram as her taxi zig-zagged up the narrow, steep streets to the top of the Peak.

But Darius would never take the tram again. Would the pain always be so sharp? Would everything remind her so vividly of him?

When the taxi stopped she looked up and saw the large white house. As she handed the driver some money, she caught a glimpse of herself in his rearview mirror and realized that Jimmy would know what was wrong just by looking at her. Her cheeks were hollow, and the skin under her eyes was a deep gray. There was no color to her face at all. Even her hair lay tangled and loose about her shoulders.

She got out of the cab, picked up her luggage and walked to Jimmy's front gate. She rang the bell. The butler, who recognized her immediately, was clearly shocked at her appearance. He took her suitcase and led her into the living room. As she sat on the sofa, he asked if she wanted something cold to drink. She just shook her head, and he left quickly.

At the sound of the hurried clicking of Jimmy's shoes on the hard-wood floors, she stood and faced him.

He stopped, his expression immobile as he studied her.

She needed to speak, but no words would come.

"What is it?" He reached for her arm and gripped it tightly, his face strained.

She blinked and looked away. He released her arm, and, as if his legs could no longer support him, sat down on the sofa.

"Tell me what happened." His voice was gentle, yet resigned, as if this were something he had been expecting.

She sat beside him. "We went to Sarawak to find the White Dragon," she began, then slowly, painfully, told him the whole story. When she finished, they sat in silence for a long time.

Jimmy clasped his hands, not moving, not looking at her. Finally he spoke, his voice strained, desperate. "I don't believe it. Darius knows how to take care of himself."

C.J. looked at him and shook her head. "Jimmy, I was there."

"I'll send a search party. Professionals. Not some villagers, do gooders and churchmen who probably couldn't find the Empire State Building if they were dropped in the middle of New York City."

She couldn't say anything, and fought against her tears.

He smashed his fist on the coffee table. She jumped at the sound. "I won't sit here and do nothing!" he shouted. The look he gave her was terrible.

He got up and stormed from the room.

She sat there until her heart stopped racing. *I'm so sorry Jimmy. So very sorry.* Darius had said they were like brothers.

She walked to the front door and picked up her suitcase.

"C.J." She heard Jimmy's choked voice behind her as she put her hand on the doorknob. She turned around.

"Please stay." He stood at the top of the landing, peering down at her. "For a little while, at least. Wait with me for word. We'll find him; I know we will."

She shook her head. "It's my fault, all of this. He went there because of me. I should just leave."

"No, C.J. Have more faith in him. I think that if Darius had a choice, he'd want you to be here. To wait, and not give up. Please... stay a while. Wait with me."

She raised her eyes.

"You're the only woman he ever brought to this house, C.J. That means a lot to me. I hope it does to you, too."

His words surprised her. She nodded. She was unable to speak, to argue with Jimmy, and she put down her suitcase. As much as she believed waiting would be fruitless, she couldn't resist the small grain of hope he offered.

CHAPTER 18

She spent her days in Jimmy's garden, painting. First she tackled the view before her, that of Hong Kong harbor.

But then she remembered Darius's last request to her, that he wanted her to paint Sarawak for him. She did. It wasn't quite as she had seen it, not like a photograph at all, but an impression of Sarawak, of the colors, the heat, the humidity, even the noise. And of her love.

When she began, she thought she would paint the desolation, the fear, the hatred she had felt, but she didn't. To her surprise, what she wanted to capture were the times of happiness, the beauty and the uniqueness of the land. It was a catharsis for her, and she wondered if Darius had somehow known it would be that way.

At first she painted quickly, needing the release of her emotions. Then, using the same raw feelings, she carefully planned the next work incorporating all the technical knowledge she had learned over the years.

The result was so good it surprised her. It was an impression, mainly in greens, blues and grays, of a rain forest. It had neither people nor animals, and was blurred, as if in a storm. The image connoted movement, life, beauty, yet also held a sense of threatening danger. The painting had a power to it that assaulted the viewer, making it hard to look away.

Jimmy often stood behind her and watched her work day after

day as she sat at the canvas. When she had almost finished the "big" picture, as she called it, he asked if he could buy it.

"No," she said.

"I'll give you top dollar," he coaxed.

"No, Jimmy." She turned to him and clasped the hand he had laid upon her shoulder, then rested it against her cheek. "If you like it, it's a present."

"I couldn't do that."

"I insist. I want you to have it."

He kissed her forehead, then went indoors again.

The searchers he had hired had been in Sarawak for over a week, but there had been no word from them. She knew this was preying on his mind. She, too, had hoped in the beginning, although she had chided herself mercilessly for her foolishness. But slowly, as they waited, as day after day went by with no news, that small hope lessened, then disappeared.

She was coming up the walk, having gone shopping for more paints, when the door to Jimmy's house burst open and he came flying down the stairs, a huge smile on his face.

She stood, open mouthed, as he approached, afraid to hope that his joy had anything to do with his best friend. But what else would make him look so thankful? No, it wasn't possible. She knew it couldn't be possible, but the name that was always on her mind slipped from her lips. "Darius?"

Jimmy wrapped his arms around her, lifted her off the ground and twirled her around, shouting, "Yes, yes," while she laughed and cried at the same time.

"Is he all right?" she asked, wiping away her tears when he put her down.

"I spoke to him. He's fine. He's in Singapore. He'll be home tomorrow."

"Thank God," she whispered as Jimmy led her inside. Soon, her questions tumbled out. "Was it your search party? Did they rescue him?"

"No. Apparently he was able to get out by himself. I don't know the details yet. He'll tell us when he's here. But he's got the White

Dragon. He found it; that's why he was gone so long. It was a long search, but he finally found it. It's what he wanted."

"Yes," she said quietly, with a half smile. "It is, isn't it? Well, I'm glad he's got it, then."

"There is one thing, though. He asks a favor of you."

"Me?"

"It won't be easy, but he said you are the only one who could 'pull it off,' so to speak."

Her eyebrows rose.

"You must go to Luchow and let the border patrol know—without actually saying so—first, that you know about Chan Li, and second, that Darius will arrive at Kai Tak airport at 1 p.m. tomorrow."

"You're kidding!" she gasped. What was Darius thinking?

Jimmy smiled and shook his head. "You know Darius and his plans."

"But how? Why?"

Jimmy just shrugged. "You'll have to figure out a good excuse, then go. It's safe, or Darius would never ask it of you."

"Do you know what's going on, Jimmy?"

"Do you imagine I understand Darius?" he countered with a smile.

Actually, she thought that if anyone understood Darius, it was Jimmy, but she also realized that if he didn't want to tell her something, no amount of prying would get it out of him. She returned his smile. Everything felt good again. She was, as usual, completely in the dark about Dangerous Kane and his plans, and she didn't care. All that mattered was that he was alive and coming back to them.

Jimmy insisted that she go to Luchow immediately and lent her his Porsche for the drive.

The Porsche was the perfect car to negotiate the tiny, twisty road down the Peak. Her heart was in her mouth as she dealt with the heavy traffic of the Wanchai area and, for the first time, drove through the Cross Harbour Tunnel. Finally she passed the city and reached the open spaces of the New Territory to head north to Luchow. She swung off the highway and pulled up in front of the police station she had come to know so well, then went into the border patrol office next door.

As she had expected, Captain Burnham was there, along with several other men. Burnham swaggered over to her.

"More missing relatives?" he asked with properly accented sarcasm.

"Not this time."

"I thought I instructed you to stay away from here."

"I'm not doing anything wrong."

"That's no assurance you'll not find yourself in further trouble."

She had forgotten how big and odious the man was. Her heart sank a little as she wondered how she could pull this off. Then she stiffened her spine and remembered the C period, J period of old, the one who bullied and blustered at the authorities when something mattered to her. She squared her shoulders and continued with her plan.

"Look, all I'm doing is trying to find a very expensive camera. A Leica. I lost it when I was here, and I was hoping you might have found it. That's all."

"Why don't you ask your bounty hunter friend? Lost and stolen goods are his specialty."

She shrugged. "I'm sure he doesn't know."

"Maybe he took it."

"If he did, I won't know that until tomorrow. And I don't want to accuse him of anything until I'm sure it's not here."

"What do you mean, tomorrow? Where is he?"

"Singapore. He won't arrive until one or so. Why do you want to know?"

Burnham looked stricken. "Actually, I don't. But if I cared about any of this, I would start with you lying to me about his identity!"

She cocked an eyebrow, putting her thumbs in her belt loops. "You know, I think it's kind of funny, the way you gave me such a hard time about my poor brother when you had an unsolved murder right under your nose!"

His lips turned thin and white. "What are you talking about?"

"Chan Li. He was killed right nearby."

"That's a police problem, not the border patrol's."

"From what I hear, Chan Li was very much a border patrol problem."

He glared at her, arms folded. "You seem to know a lot about Chan Li."

"Just that he was a smuggler and someone killed him right here in Luchow."

"And about the White Dragon?"

"No."

"You're not a good liar, Miss Perkins."

She backed toward the door, fearful she might have gone too far. "I take it you haven't found my camera," she said. "Good day, Captain Burnham." She hurried from the station, mission accomplished.

As she drove back to Jimmy's house, she tried to understand what was going on, but none of it made sense to her.

Chan Li was a thief and with other men he had stolen the White Dragon. He double-crossed his fellow thieves, tried to kill them, and hid the White Dragon in a grandfather clock in Luchow. There, he was killed.

One of the other thieves, a pirate, lived long enough to tell her brother Alan where the Dragon was hidden. Alan went to Luchow, stole the Dragon himself, then hid it in Sarawak as he tried to find a buyer.

So who had killed Chan Li?

As Alan tried to find a buyer, he made himself a target of other thieves as well as the police. He learned that the mysterious Mr. Yeng in San Francisco would pay a small fortune for the Dragon and went there to sell it. But Yeng turned out to be too dangerous a man for Alan to deal with. What was Yeng's role in all this?

And Darius—Darius made no sense at all. She was sure that meeting him in Luchow had been an accident, and that Burnham hadn't known who Darius was at the time. But he did know that Darius wasn't Alan Perkins.

Captain Burnham surely knew by now that Darius was a bounty hunter. So why did Darius now want the Luchow border patrol to know he would soon be back in Hong Kong?

Somewhere there had to be an answer, a link that would tie everything together in a way that made sense.

It was evening before she reached Hong Kong Island again. As she drove up the Peak to Jimmy's house, she looked out at the harbor. Hong Kong had never looked lovelier. The lights were aglow on the island and across the harbor on Kowloon. Even the boats in the water were lit up.

She recognized the romantic Star Ferry slowly making its way across the channel; maybe she would ride it someday with Darius. It seemed as if the very air were filled with laughter and music.

And no matter what he was up to, she loved Darius.

oOo

The next morning, Jimmy said she should wait at the house while he went to pick up Darius at the airport. She was shocked and tried to protest, but he wouldn't listen, saying he had to stop off at his office first, and that she would be bored. Then he left.

C.J. walked around the house, around the garden, then around the house again. She didn't know what to do with herself. It was only eleven o'clock. She had been pacing since eight.

She changed her clothes three times. She was disgusted at how plain and drab her clothes were. Why didn't she ever buy red? She finally settled on dark blue slacks, blue sandals with little heels, a blue-and-white striped blouse and a white jacket. They hung loosely on her, startling her by how much weight she'd lost the past few weeks.

Darius's plane was arriving at one. Jimmy would pick him up, and he could be home as early as one-thirty. No, two o'clock was more likely. Wait! He had the jade with him.

He'd have to turn it in to Customs at the airport. There would be a lot of questions; he'd have to make depositions.

It could take hours. And he'd be alone, except for Jimmy.

But she was the one who had gotten him into this, so why shouldn't she be there with him, to help with the explanations? To hold his hand, if she couldn't help in any other way.

She picked up her bag and jacket. No wonder Jimmy had thought she should wait at the house. He was, as usual, more concerned about her physical comfort than her emotional state. He thought she might get tired or bored. Silly man! How could she be either as long as Darius was near?

She took the tram down the hill and was at the airport by twelve-thirty.

The gate where the plane from Singapore would be arriving was easy to find. She still had at least twenty minutes to wait, and once the plane landed, it would take a while before Darius went through Customs.

A gift shop was nearby. It was worth a visit. Maybe she could find something Darius would like. She was walking toward the shop when someone slipped his hand onto her arm, hurrying her away from the arrival gate.

She spun around to look into a familiar face. The man had white hair and pale blue eyes. She remembered him—Robert Davis, the British intelligence agent.

He nodded, his face stern, and continued leading her away. "Miss Perkins, I must ask you to stay away from this area." His tone was quiet, matter-of-fact. They didn't miss a step as they walked.

"But?" Her heart sank. Of course—Darius. He was the reason the agents were there. Did they know about the White Dragon? That Darius had it? But how could they?

"Will you do as I say? It may not be safe, considering some of the people you do—and do not—know." She was confused by his words. People she didn't know? Who? What were they planning to do?

"What do you mean?" She stopped walking, ready to plead, beg, anything to have him tell her what was at the bottom of this. "Please, tell me."

"In good time, my dear." He patted her hand. "In good time. Now, just wait anywhere around here. I'll know how to find you."

Like hell I will, she thought, watching his retreating figure. She went into the largest tourist shop she could find and picked out an orange, floppy-brimmed sun hat. She tried it on. The brim covered most of her face. She decided to tuck her hair up under it. "Do you sell hair bands and hatpins?" C.J. asked the saleswoman. She didn't want the hat to fall off.

"Barrettes and elastic hairbands are over there. But hatpins? Oh, I know what you mean. The only ones we have are these souvenirs." She pointed to a display that had been pushed far to the back of the counter.

C.J. picked one up. It was long, with a red-and white HOORAY FOR HONG KONG flag attached to the top of it. "I'll take it." She added a hair band, and then glanced at the clothes. In for a penny, she thought as she reached for a tight rather low-cut pink T-shirt with Hong Kong emblazoned on it, snug jeans, and oversized sunglasses. At the last minute, she added red lipstick.

With a grimace, she pulled out her money. She was truly desperate.

In the women's room, she put on her new clothes, stashing her old "sensible" outfit in the shopping bag. She had never worn anything quite so sexy and figure-hugging.

As she passed by a shop window, she caught a glimpse of herself. With a start, she saw that she looked completely different from the way she had a few minutes ago when Davis talked to her. Even Mildred wouldn't recognize me, she thought, and marched toward the gate.

It was almost time for the plane to appear. She lingered in the back of the arrival area, where she could see everyone.

She knew that the British agents were there somewhere, but they had managed to disappear. She looked over the crowd, then gasped. An Oriental man, the one she had hit with the mallet at Yeng's place, stood among the people who had assembled to meet the flight. What was he doing here?

He was with some other men, none of whom she recognized. And there was Jimmy, off in a corner, nonchalantly reading *The Wall Street Journal.* How like him!

She turned back to Yeng's men. Why were they here? How could they have known Darius was coming? Unless. . . no, he wouldn't have told them. Jimmy wouldn't have. Darius had joked about selling the jade to them, but he wouldn't really do that. He wasn't that way. Alan, her own brother, was. . . but not Darius.

The plane's arrival was announced. She saw it roll toward the gate. Soon Darius would come through the jetway, and be greeted by customs officials. He would give them the White Dragon and then all this would be over. She knew it. She absolutely knew it.

The first passengers started to pass through the customs check, then more of them. Yeng's men moved toward the gate. C.J. saw Robert Davis in the far corner of the waiting area. She knew his men couldn't be far away.

Most of the passengers had gone through customs and were already heading out of the airport. Where was Darius? What was wrong?

Then she saw him. He was calmly walking off the plane with his usual lithe grace, carrying a small satchel. He was dressed as casually as ever in white slacks, a powder-blue T-shirt, a loose-fitting khaki jacket and aviator-style sun glasses. She couldn't stop herself from smiling, or stop the sudden wetness of her eyes.

He raised his head, as if taking in the whole room from behind his dark glasses.

She stepped a little closer, watching him intently as he neared the customs inspector. It was time for him to turn over the White Dragon.

He shook his head in response to a couple of questions.

Darius, tell him about the jade. Now. It's time. Please, Darius, tell him. She watched expectantly. Her hands curled into fists as she watched his every movement. Her whole body throbbed. *Tell him, Darius, please tell him! You can't come through customs with stolen goods. You have to tell them about the Dragon!* She wanted to run to him, to take the Dragon away from him and turn it over, to get it out of their lives.

God, please! Don't let him smuggle it into Hong Kong.

But Darius wouldn't do that, she decided. He couldn't. He must have a plan. Darius always had plans.

The customs inspector waved him through. Darius picked up his bag and smiled as he stepped into the waiting area of the airport. Still smiling, he walked toward Yeng's men, and then nodded.

CHAPTER 19

The world began to spin. Black and purple spots flashed
before her eyes, making it seem she was looking at Darius
through a blinking strobe light. She took off the sun glasses, and they
slid from her hand onto the ground.

Robert Davis and the British police moved toward the small
group. They were going to be arrested, Darius and Yeng's men, in
connection with the White Dragon theft. Jimmy Lee saw what was
happening and backed away, fading into a group of travelers.

How had she been so wrong about Darius? Once she had believed
in her brother, but he deceived her. Then she had wanted to believe
in Darius, and now this….

She was stupid! A stupid, gullible fool!

She couldn't stay and watch him get arrested. She found herself
moving, stumbling backward, then running, needing to get away.

Her eyes were blinded by harsh, burning tears as she ran to the
exit, then out onto the parking lot. She bumped into people. Her hat
fell off; she picked it up and continued running. The shopping bag
with her old clothes was knocked from her hand by the crowd, then
kicked aside, out of reach.

She didn't care; she simply hurried on, needing to get away, far,
far away. Away from her thoughts, from her disappointment, from
her own heart.

"Hey there!" a familiar voice called out. She looked in the direction it had come from. It was Captain Burnham from Luchow, heading toward her. "Do you need a ride?"

She ran to him—anything to get away from this place.

"I say, are you all right?" he asked as she got into the car.

"Yes. I will be."

"Fine." He turned flipped on the police siren and, magically, the other cars moved out of his way.

She became calmer. He handed her his large handkerchief, and she dried her eyes. "Thank you," she whispered.

"It's nothing." He switched off the siren now that they were clear of the traffic jam around the airport.

"I guess you're heading back to Luchow," she said. "You can drop me off anywhere you want. I'll get a taxi."

"No problem. Where are you going?" He gave her a quizzical glance as he steered through the traffic.

"I'm... I was staying with a friend at the Peak. I'm going to go back there, pack, and head for home. Back to Los Angeles"

"Very wise decision. I was going that way myself. To Hong Kong Island, I mean. I can drive you."

"You were going to Hong Kong Island?"

"Yes. To Repulse Bay. I have a boat there. It's a lovely spot, quiet— very British, in fact. You wouldn't even know you were in Hong Kong."

He entered heavy traffic as he made his way through the heart of Kowloon. A flip of the switch started his siren again, and like the waves parting for Moses, the cars pulled aside to let him through.

"That's a nice gadget," she said. "I'll have to get one for the L.A. freeways."

He laughed.

"A boat," she murmured, doing all she could to concentrate on anything but Darius and what was happening to him. "I've often wondered what it's like to live on a boat. When things get rough, to just pull up anchor and drift away..." Her eyes inexplicably filled with tears again.

They reached the Cross Harbour Tunnel. The entrance, dipping under the water, looked like a great, gaping mouth.

The water of the harbor above it was like a wide, blue mustache, and the Peak formed a giant nose. She always felt uneasy in the Tunnel, knowing there were millions of tons of water above her.

"You'll come with me," he said.

"Come with you? To Repulse Bay? I'm afraid I don't have time today. You can let me out anywhere here," she said as they reached the Wanchai area of Hong Kong Island.

"You don't understand, Miss Perkins. I'm not asking you to join me, I'm telling you."

"What?" She looked at him as if he were joking.

"This is not a game. I need you as insurance." He kept his eyes on the traffic while speaking to her completely calmly.

"Insurance? For what?" The man irritated her; he was always acting so pompous. Whatever was he talking about now?

"To get away, of course. I need to go to Macao, where I'll be safe. With my gun aimed at you, I won't be stopped—unless the police here don't care if a young American woman is killed. Luckily for you, they do care."

She looked at him as if he were crazy. He was a British border official; what kind of gibberish was he speaking?

Nothing made sense to her anymore. "I don't understand—"

"I'm talking about jade, Miss Perkins! The White Dragon, to be precise. And Mr. Yeng—my boss."

She gasped sharply and turned to him, a shocked look on her face.

"Yes." He smiled. "Now it begins to make sense, doesn't it? Mr. Yeng wants the Dragon. He wants it very badly, so badly he even had me kill Chan Li to get it. Now do you understand?"

"You?" She was shocked.

"Of course. Who else could have gotten through Chan Li's bodyguards? They all trusted me. Chan Li and I worked together on a number of deals over the years. Luchow was a convenient place for that. Poor man, he trusted me."

None of this made sense. "You killed Chan Li? Why didn't you take the Dragon?"

Burnham's face darkened.

She snickered. "Don't tell me you couldn't find it!"

"I searched everywhere! It wasn't until you showed up that I had any clue as to what might have happened to it."

She looked at him with horror. "My brother..."

Burnham pounded the steering wheel with each word. "I don't understand how he found it when I couldn't. We searched for him, then when you showed up, we wasted time searching your things, both in Hong Kong and then in Los Angeles. But then Alan Perkins found his way to San Francisco and the big man himself." He chuckled. "I used my position to have him detained, but once Yeng captured you, we assumed Perkins would go straight to him to free you. I telephoned San Francisco, told them Perkins was innocent. What I don't understand, is why your brother didn't go straight to Yeng at that point."

She laughed, a high hysterical laugh. "And if he had?"

"That's simple. We'd have the Dragon, and you'd have a corpse."

"God! You're despicable."

"Actually, I'm a rather nice fellow. But anyway, when we heard you and Kane were in Sarawak, we knew you had to be looking for the jade."

"You heard? How could you have heard that?"

"Why, from our co-worker, of course. John Carter. Surely you remember him? Nice chap, isn't he?"

Carter. So that explained his behavior, his strange questions.

"Carter was convinced you didn't have the Dragon. Believe me, if you'd had it, he would have known. He thought you really believed Kane was dead. No one could be that good an actress, he told us. I guess you did believe it. Kane really used you, didn't he?"

She set her jaw and glared at him. The man was horrid, absolutely hateful. Then he laughed. He threw back his head and laughed at her. She reached for the door handle to open it, to get out of the car. She didn't care how fast they were going, she didn't care what happened to her, all she wanted was to get out of the car, away from this horrible man and his lies.

With one hand he grabbed her hair and jerked her toward him. She flailed at him, and he shoved her against the passenger door as easily as if she were a child. After her shoulder and head hit, she didn't move for a moment, stunned at how strong the man was. For the first time she began to feel really afraid of him.

Burnham pulled out his gun and held it in front of her face. She sat up and remained still beside him. Her heart raced.

"That's better. Now, don't move while I drive. We're almost there."

"Why are you running now?" she asked. "Why aren't you with your friends, meeting Darius and getting the White Dragon?"

"With British agents crawling out of the woodwork? Do you think I don't know Robert Davis? Of course I do. I'm leaving the colony because I can't trust those San Francisco friends of Yeng to keep quiet about me! The Dragon is lost to us; I can see that. But Yeng has lots of friends in Macao. So I'm going there, and now, with you as insurance, I'll arrive safely."

He pulled off the highway onto a private dirt road. The road wasn't very long; and the area seemed quite deserted.

There were a few trees, lots of bushes and a small house. A short distance from the house was a dock, with what looked like a two-man fishing boat beside it. Burnham drove up to the dock and stopped the car. Despite her fear, her thoughts raced.

She had to get away. Once the madman was safely on his boat, he might realize he didn't need his "insurance" any longer.

He opened his door and stepped out of the car, then turned back and grabbed her arm. She stiffened, clutching her hat to her breast, willing herself to be strong. He pulled, dragging her across the car seat and against the steering wheel until she fell out of the car onto the gravel.

She landed in a heap and remained there, willing to do anything to stall him, to buy time to formulate a plan, to pray for a miracle. In the past she would have counted on Darius. Now, she knew that was impossible. She clung tenaciously to the ground.

"Get up!" He nudged her with the toe of his shoe.

She didn't move.

She heard a click and raised her head. The gun was aimed right at her.

"I said, get up," he repeated.

Slowly, she rose. She picked up her hat, but looked all over the ground.

"Now what?" Burnham demanded.

"My purse. I must have left it in the car." She started back.

Burnham grabbed her arm and spun her around toward the boat. "Move!" he yelled. "You won't need any damned handbag where you're going!"

"But I—"

He jabbed the gun into her back. Slowly, she started to walk. He grabbed her left arm from behind, holding her in front of him. With the gun in his right hand, he prodded her to an ever faster pace. They were almost at the wooden dock. The distance to the boat looked far too short for comfort.

Her feet dragged as she wracked her brain for some way to save herself. The cold metal of the gun was like dry ice against her back. One foot stepped onto the dock.

"Drop, C.J.!" It was Darius! For a split second she froze, then threw herself toward the ground—too late.

Burnham's grip tightened on her arm, and he spun her around in front of him. He held her between himself and Darius, using her to protect him from the .357 Magnum that was aimed at his chest. She twisted this way and that, and as she did, she pulled out her hatpin, holding it tightly in her right hand. It was the only "weapon" she possessed. She stopped struggling as she felt Burnham's gun against her temple. His arm wrapped around her like a python, crushing her ribs, pinning her arms to her sides, making it almost impossible for her to breathe. She was held against his left side, and his right hand was holding the gun.

She saw Darius facing them in a half crouch, his gun still aimed at Burnham. She hadn't seen or heard Jimmy Lee and prayed he was somewhere nearby.

"Not clever enough, Kane," Burnham shouted. "Not fast enough, either. Throw down your gun."

Darius looked at C.J. With Burnham's gun so close to her, she knew there was nothing Darius could do. "Why?" Darius shouted. "So you can shoot me? There's no benefit to me in that, Burnham. Let her go. Then get on your boat and leave."

"As you said, 'no benefit to me in that,'" Burnham shouted.

Burnham began to walk backward up the gangplank, holding C.J. so tight she could scarcely breathe, half dragging her with him towards the boat. Darius watched, his frustration thick in the air.

There was only one hope. She maneuvered the hatpin so that the round, plastic head was by her thumb, the shaft against her palm. About two inches protruded past her little finger to the sharp point.

She turned her head ever so slightly to look at Burnham's body. She knew she would have only one chance. She couldn't afford to hit a zipper; the hatpin wasn't strong enough for that.

The pounding of her heart jarred her whole body. She swallowed hard. Should she try it? Was there any other way? The hatpin seemed so fragile. Could she risk her life on it? A few more steps and she'd be on the boat, escape almost impossible. If she were going to act, it had to be now.

She lifted her hand slightly, then drove it down hard into him. The hatpin hit its mark perfectly, and a strange, gurgling high-pitched shriek escaped Burnham as his whole body jerked.

The shock and pain caused Burnham's arms to spasmodically jerk, loosening his hold. The instant he did, she hurled herself off the dock into the water. As she went over, a shot rang out. She heard Burnham's body fall.

She stood, wringing wet, as Darius and Jimmy ran toward her, Jimmy with a gun still in his hand. The water was only up to her waist, but it felt slimy and filthy, and she couldn't stop shaking. Darius gave her his hand to pull her out and into his arms. Jimmy ran up the dock to the boat.

"What did you do to him?" Darius asked, brushing her wet hair off her face. "I never heard a man sound like that."

"Look!" Jimmy pointed. C.J. was astonished to see Jimmy's complexion turn slightly green as he spun away from Burnham's body.

Darius followed Jimmy's pointing finger. Burnham lay sprawled out on his back, the hatpin still protruding from where she had placed it, HOORAY FOR HONG KONG, prominently displayed.

"Oooh, C.J...." Darius shuddered.

She stepped back, looking from one man to the other, then folded her arms and shook her head. "He's lying there with a hole in his shoulder, and you're like two big babies over a hat pin? I don't believe it!"

As Darius looked at her, a smile slowly curved his lips. He wrapped an arm around her shoulder and led her away from the dock to the hillside where his gun lay. "Are you okay, Cleo? I keep forgetting that you're one woman who doesn't need rescuing."

"I'm okay." She smiled back, then her face crumbled in tears. "Oh, Darius, I was so worried about you!"

He crushed her against him, kissing her until she was sure the heat from her body would dry her clothes instantaneously.

"Plenty of time for that later, you two," Jimmy called. "Here come more police. We've got more explaining to do."

When the police arrived, Darius asked them to release C.J. He told them that this was a complicated situation, and that they should call headquarters. They did, and were quickly instructed to do as requested. As C.J. was put into one car, and Darius and Jimmy into another, she was still trying to get answers to her many questions, but to no avail.

She was driven away without a word.

CHAPTER 20

The police drove her straight to Jimmy Lee's house without asking a single question. It was baffling.

Jimmy's butler stood open-mouthed as he watched her step out of the police car, then enter the house, wringing wet and smelling of fish and salt water.

She went to her room to shower and change, forcing herself to go through the motions and not think about anything else.

It was only afterward, as she stood alone on the deck at the side of Jimmy's home overlooking the harbor, that she let herself go. It was as if she had opened the floodgates; all the thoughts she had been suppressing came washing over her.

How had Darius gotten out of Sarawak? How had he gotten free of Robert Davis and the British agents? Of Yeng's men? He must be working for the British, she concluded.

But if he was, they wouldn't have been questioning her about him earlier, and he would have contacted them in San Francisco.

No, as soon as she thought about it, she knew she was wrong. Whatever the reason he had been let through at the airport, it wasn't because he was an agent. He had been after the White Dragon reward. Of that, she was certain.

Or was she?

She slowly stormed around the deck rubbing her arms.

He had been lucky this time, she thought; he could so easily have been killed in Sarawak or at the airport. By Yeng's men; by the police. But Darius always had plans. He was smug about them. Too smug, she feared.

She would never forget the look on Jimmy's face when she had told him that Darius was dead. There had been pain, sorrow—but no surprise. In fact, it had almost been as if he were expecting it.

A shudder rippled through her. He had been lucky this time, but what about the next time?

What treasure would he go after next? And with what result?

Darius, give this up, she pleaded silently. *Please give this up!*

She felt as if she were going mad. Her thoughts rushed around in her head, bumping into each other. She shut her eyes and placed her fingertips on her temples, rubbing them, trying to drive the madness away.

She loved him. But was that enough?

She rose and went indoors to the music room. She sat on one of the chairs facing the grand piano.

It took a special kind of woman to live with a man who constantly faced danger. It was one thing to stay with a man who lived that way because it was his work and he believed in it, like a policeman. But a man who lived that way because he couldn't face the way his life had become, because he was running away from tragedy. It was no way to live. Instinctively, she knew Darius realized it, but he also didn't know how to stop himself.

The situation was all wrong. She walked through the house to the deck, watching what seemed like half the world pass below her, as thoughts of Darius swirled in her head.

Over three hours had passed, and during every minute she had wondered whether he had been arrested. Finally she heard the car pull into the garage.

She ran to the hallway, watching the entrance from the garage in anxious anticipation.

The door opened, and Darius stepped into the house, home again.

"Thank God," she whispered, not moving as he rushed to her, smiling broadly. He threw his arms around her waist and spun her around.

"C.J., we've got it! We've got the reward!"

He put her down and stepped back to look at her, still holding her waist, his face glowing. She placed her hands on his arms as her lungs seemed to constrict, cutting off her breath. His first words had been about the reward. That told her everything she needed to know. She stepped back, away from him.

"It's ours! And it's huge!" He moved closer.

"I see."

"Did you hear me?" Perplexity, then disbelief, filled his eyes.

"Yes. It's good, Darius. You did well."

"It'll take a week or so to get it, but your share—"

She shook her head. "I don't want it." She tried to smile at him, to look happy. "I was never in this for the reward. I don't want money from you. You earned it; you deserve it."

He didn't move. "You make it sound like there's something wrong with it."

"No. Not at all. I just..." She looked at him again. Her heart melted. She couldn't talk about the reward. Not now. He was with her; he was alive! That was all that really mattered. "Darius, I'm so glad you're home." The words didn't begin to express the way she felt.

He said nothing, but stared silently at her as he placed his hands on her waist again. She rubbed his shoulders, then lifted her hands to his handsome face, assuring herself that he was really with her now, for this moment. But soon, she knew, the moment would end.

She brushed a lock of hair back from his forehead. "Are you all right? How did you get away from those headhunters, or whatever they were?"

He took her hand, kissed her palm, then continued to hold it. "Do you remember the villagers who were going on a hunting trip when we were there?"

She remembered every detail of those days. "Yes."

"I got them to work for me," he said. "They were the 'headhunters.'"

She felt the blood drain from her face.

His hands tightened their hold, his voice was calm as he continued. "They helped me find the White Dragon and make my way through the jungle, using the rivers. There's an immense network of waterways. They helped me quite a bit. You and I could never have made it alone, C.J. That was very clear to me."

"I don't understand." Her eyes never left his.

"The problem was John Carter. As soon as I saw him there, I realized he had to be working for Yeng. I had to get the White Dragon out of the country without returning to Bir Sakan, and I had to get you out, too. Once I saw that we were in danger, I had to change our plans."

"Why didn't you tell me?" She couldn't believe he had been so thoughtless, so cruel.

"I had to get you out of there." He rubbed her waist, his thumbs moving upward, playing with her ribcage. "My biggest worry was that you'd figure out that Carter was an impostor. The man was such a fool, he nearly gave himself away a couple of times. Your only chance to escape him was your innocence."

"My innocence! That's why you left me?" She pushed him away, stopping his caresses.

He looked at her, puzzled. "I knew Carter wouldn't let anything happen to you as long as he believed you knew nothing about all this. It's easy to tell the Malay government a man went off into the jungle and disappeared. It's not that unusual. But a woman, especially one whose brother was involved in the theft of a major art treasure, could cause a huge investigation. He wouldn't want that."

She turned her back on him, not able to look at him, not wanting him to touch her. "I see. For the sake of this jade, you faked your death. You didn't tell me or Jimmy, knowing how we feel about you, knowing how we would suffer." Her throat tightened, stopping her words as the agony she felt came back to her anew.

"I told Jimmy as soon as I could!" His voice was harsh. "And I didn't fake my death! I told you I'd be all right. I told you to trust me. You were the one who decided I was dead! As far as I was concerned, I was just missing. Don't you understand, woman? I wanted you to be safe! It would have been dangerous, maybe impossible, to get you out alive with Carter there once we found the Dragon!"

"The Dragon..." She nodded. "Funny, I've never even seen what it looks like."

She walked to the living room and sat on a chair facing the large picture window.

Darius followed her and stood behind her. "C.J.! It's what we were there for!"

Her gaze was veiled. "Yes. Of course."

"I didn't think it would make any difference—"

"Oh, Darius!" she cried in dismay as she bent forward, her head in her hands.

"I don't understand you!" He stormed to her side, lifted her off the chair, and made her look at him, holding her arms. "We did what we set out to do and you're upset? This is supposed to be a celebration, not a funeral. This is the biggest thing that's ever happened to me. It's fantastic!"

"Congratulations."

He let go of her. "Is that all you can say? I got us a fortune and saved your brother's worthless neck, and that's all you have to say about it?"

"I'm sorry." She turned her head aside, biting her bottom lip.

"Sorry? Look at me!" he shouted. "What do I have to do next time? Find the stash from the Great Train Robbery?"

Next time!

He had said it. Her body suddenly felt rigid, as if all the life had gone out of it and all that was left was a hard shell.

Next time...

It was as if she were looking at him through the wrong end of a telescope. Everything went black around him, and he suddenly seemed very small and far away.

She couldn't stay there any longer; she couldn't bear it. She took a step away from him, then another, and somehow she managed to cross the room to the door.

He made a move in her direction and held out his hand, but then stopped and let his hand fall to his side.

She would never forget him standing there, looking so lost, so hurt. She wanted to run back to him and hold him.

But he had told her in Singapore that he didn't want her with him.

In Sarawak, he called himself a bastard and said it was wrong for him to make love to her.

And then he had left her.

Even now, he continued to choose a life she could never be a part of. And he knew it; he knew it. She felt as if her heart had been taken from her body, laid at his feet, and then kicked aside. Ever since their talk in Singapore, she had known the time would come to leave.

But the knowing and the doing were so very different....

She stopped at the doorway, then with her hand against the doorjamb as if for support, she turned and looked at him one last time. "It's Clothilde," she said. "Clothilde Jane Perkins. Good-bye, Darius."

Jimmy was waiting for her in the entry hall as she left the guest room with her packed bag. He took her suitcase and placed it on the floor.

"Stay, C.J. You two can work things out."

"It's no good, Jimmy. We're too different. We don't believe in the same things—basic things, like what's really important in life." She blinked hard; she wouldn't let him see her tears. "Take care of him, Jimmy."

"I will."

She hugged him. He held her close and patted her back.

"I'll drive you," he said. "And maybe convince you not to go."

"I'll accept the ride."

She looked up at the house as they got into the car. Darius was standing at the window watching them, a bitter, stricken look on his face. She turned away.

As the Porsche descended the Peak, she found her voice again. "I never did hear how Darius got free at the airport. I thought he would be arrested."

"It was a setup," Jimmy replied nonchalantly.

"What?"

"Once Darius got the Dragon, he wanted to get the men behind the whole thing, too. After he learned that Chan Li had not only lived in Luchow but had been involved in smuggling, what better place to look for a link between him and Yeng than the border patrol? Darius asked me to alert British intelligence about his plan. That was also why you had to ask the border patrol about Chan Li and let them know Darius would be returning. If Darius's guess was right, Yeng's contact in the border patrol would alert him that Darius, and most likely the Dragon, would be at the airport this afternoon. When they saw him 'smuggle' it into the country and approach them, they thought he was willing to negotiate with them. That's when British intelligence stepped in and made some arrests.

"Luckily, that ridiculous hat you wore didn't hide from me who you were, and when I saw you run, I realized you thought Darius was also arrested. I spotted Burnham from a window, and got Darius away from the police as fast as I could. That siren of Burnham's gave us a good idea where he was, even when we couldn't see the car for all the traffic. And, of course, Darius can drive through Hong Kong traffic like no one else I've ever seen."

C.J. sat mutely as Jimmy gave her the explanation. "Will Yeng also be arrested?" she asked when he had finished.

"I don't know about Yeng. He's in San Francisco, and very powerful. But at least his Hong Kong connection is broken up. It's a start. It's up to U.S. agents now, the FBI and Customs."

"Good."

They rode on in silence, until Jimmy drove up to the entrance to the terminal. He helped carry her bags to the airline counter. "Are you sure, C.J.? Won't you stay for a little while, at least?"

"I can't compete with Asia, Jimmy. But thank you." She kissed him on the cheek, and he squeezed her hand in encouragement.

"Goodbye, C.J.," he said.

"Goodbye," she whispered, then watched him leave the terminal to return to his home—and Darius.

An hour later she was in the plane, soaring high over Hong Kong. The colony looked so small from the sky, but it was full of life and people, and, to her, it was the most beautiful place on earth. She watched until it disappeared over the horizon.

Her eyes remained dry. Some emotions were beyond tears.

CHAPTER 21

*O*nly by looking at the calendar did C.J. know that summer and fall had come and gone and that it was now winter, because the weather in Los Angeles went from warm to hot to simply warm again as the year progressed.

She was working in her apartment, wearing jeans and a red tank top as evening approached. She wore lots of red now, ignoring the beiges, blues and pastels she used to wear. It was Thursday, the night Muldoon's Bar and Grill had its big pasta party, but she hadn't attended since she'd returned from Hong Kong.

She put down her paintbrush and palette and wiped her hands with a rag, careful not to bump into any of the paintings that cluttered her small living space. The last few months of the tourist season had been lucrative, almost exclusively due to the popularity of her Sarawak scenes—especially the ones that included a man with sun-streaked hair and green eyes.

A half-finished painting of him stood on her easel.

As she critically eyed her work, there was a knock on the door. Tossing aside the rag, she crossed the room with irritation—it was probably a salesman—and pulled open the door. Everything within her stopped.

His hair was longer than the last time she'd seen him, and he was far too thin. The tan had faded just a little. His clothes were, as usual, soft and invitingly casual—a sky-blue cotton shirt, with the sleeves rolled to his elbows, and light gray slacks.

She felt her body go warm, then cold, and her breath caught in her throat. She had longed to see him again so many times that for him to be here now, before her, was simply overwhelming.

As he watched her, his eyes sparkled. "May I come in?"

His words jarred her from her astonishment, and she waved toward the studio, then quickly raked her fingers through her hair and tugged at the bottom of her tank top to smooth it.

He entered the room and immediately crossed to the painting she was working on. He studied it for a moment. "It's good, C.J. You've got a real gift."

She couldn't seem to find her voice and made no reply.

"I saw the picture you did at Jimmy's," he continued. "It was magnificent. I'm glad you gave it to him."

She waved her arms vaguely, then tucked her fingers into her back pockets. "If I have to feel like that before I can paint a great picture," she said, her voice husky, "I hope I never do another one." She had intended it to be a joke, but it fell flat.

He stepped close to her. "I missed you, C.J. I had to see you again. How are you?"

She swallowed hard, feeling a sudden pressure behind her eyes. "I'm fine."

"Happy?"

She shrugged. "I'm doing all right."

"Seeing anyone? Engaged?"

She shook her head. "How's Jimmy?" she asked, needing to change the subject, needing to calm the emotion that swelled within her.

He took her hand, making her heart do cartwheels. "Jimmy's same as ever."

She still adored him, she realized ruefully. She hadn't been with him for two seconds before she knew it, even after all that had happened, and all the months that had passed. He had walked into her life again, and she was lost. But why? she wondered. Why was he here? She was afraid to ask, but she had to.

"And you?" she asked, pulling her hand free as she crossed to the sofa and sat down. He followed and sat beside her, too close. She shifted away from him, trying to keep her voice non-committal, casual, as she asked her, "What brings you to these shores?"

"I'm working."

"Ah. I see. On a hot pursuit for missing treasure?"

"No."

"No?"

He shook his head. "You believed in my talent, Cleo. Even though my technique was no longer perfect, you said the inspiration was there, and that I could still play. When I was at the piano, you told me I was complete, and away from it, just a shadow of myself. You were right.

"After you left I practiced eight, ten, twelve hours a day for over three months, until I felt I was ready. I went to New York, found my old agent and told him I wanted to play again. Not solo—I'm no fool. But with an orchestra—just to perform again, for nothing more than the joy of making music."

She saw the enthusiasm that lit up his face, a look she hadn't seen before. She nodded.

"I was overwhelmed, and humbled, too, by the response. A number of orchestras asked for me—good ones. And we've gotten requests for me to be the accompanist at some pretty impressive recitals. I don't know about accepting those. Maybe in time. But not yet. One step at a time, as they say."

"I'm glad. That's wonderful news." She felt proud of him, and perhaps just a little sad. He wouldn't need her nagging him to play anymore, and she was afraid that was the only way he had ever needed her, even if he hadn't known it.

"Since I was in New York," he began, his expression changing, becoming more guarded as he spoke, "I did what I should have done a long time ago. I went to see Alicia. You can't imagine what it's like to meet a little girl—she just turned six—and know she's your daughter. It's frightening, yet kind of miraculous. She's a funny kid, though. Ever since she turned four she's been saving all the gifts I sent her for her birthday and Christmas. She didn't even play with them, just put them on a shelf." He paused, his voice choked as he added, "They were her daddy, she said. That's all she had of me, and she didn't want them to get 'wrecked.'"

He stopped speaking. His eyes were misty and he quickly dropped his gaze. "Do you know how that made me feel? I thought she might hate me for having left her—but all she offered was love. No blame, no recriminations. She simply accepted me, and then...and then asked me not to go far away again." He shut his eyes a moment. "If man could stop time like film in a camera, rewind it, and shoot the scenes another way, I would have found some way to do it for her. To make it up to her."

"I know," she whispered. "All the time wasted…"

He studied her a moment before he said, "Nadia loves Alicia very much, but she's got her career, and a new husband. She travels a lot. That's what helped me decide what to do. I took a position in New York. That way I can be with my daughter. I discussed it with Nadia, and we came to an agreement. She has Alicia's best interests at heart, and, she could see that this was important to her."

"So it's all worked out for you." C.J. clasped her hands on her lap. His music and his child, he had everything he wanted. "I always did say you were a lucky man," she said a little wistfully.

"Almost." He raised his chin. "There's one more little matter."

"Which is?"

"The reward money." One of his eyebrows rose as he studied her reaction.

That money was still a bitter subject for her. She was surprised to find that it still made her stomach churn to hear about it.

He continued. "You know the way I was living before you met me, C.J. But I want you to know I never did anything I'm ashamed of, no matter what scurrilous tales you heard from British inspectors who were trying to upset you and get information out of you."

She nodded in silence, not looking at him.

"You and I did what we set out to do," he said. "We turned the White Dragon over to the Chinese government so that Alan would be out of danger. We did it, and were given a substantial reward for it." He stopped speaking and looked at her, his expression deadly serious now, his eyes searching. "I came here to ask you to forgive me. If you can, if you ever can."

She looked at him in confusion. "Forgive you?"

"For not trusting you."

"You didn't trust me?" That made no sense to her.

He stood and went to the easel to look at her painting, then paced around the room. "I spent years, C.J., telling myself that I couldn't trust anyone, except maybe Jimmy. But certainly not a woman, not ever again. I spent years telling myself that the only thing that was important was to get rich, by whatever means—legal means—it took. And what I did, I did by myself, without a care for anyone else."

"I see," she whispered.

"I didn't want to consider how you would feel if you thought I was captured by headhunters, or lost in the jungle, or—yes, I'll admit it— or dead. Oh, I thought you'd be upset for a while, but that's all. I wouldn't let myself think about it. Not after my experience with my ex-wife. But you're nothing like her; you're probably the most unselfish person I've ever met."

She was speechless; she should have realized the depth of his pain and that his inability to trust couldn't be wiped out in a few weeks. There was so much she should have realized.

"What I did was wrong, and I'm sorry, so very sorry, for hurting you." He faced her. "In Sarawak, before I went into hiding, I should have told you. I should have realized what a good actress you can be if you need to. For instance, that last afternoon in Jimmy's house, you really let me have it. I thought you hated me. Never wanted to see me again. It took Jimmy a long time to convince me I was wrong."

"Did it?" A smile played across her lips. Thank you, Jimmy Lee, she thought.

He bent to meet her at eye level. "C.J., half of that reward is yours."

The words cut through her. The reward—that damned money. That was the reason he was here. He had pulled his life together, and now he was feeling guilty about keeping what he thought belonged to her. She felt numb. She stood, pushing past him to walk to the window, then stared out at the cars going by. "I told you once I didn't want it," she whispered. "I meant it!"

"I came here to give it to you," he said.

She shut her eyes for a moment and shook her head. "I don't want money from you." Her voice was only a whisper.

He walked to her side. "I came here to ask you if you would be willing to take it if it weren't divided between us."

Her brow furrowed slightly, but she made no other movement. He hurried on.

"If, instead of splitting it, it were used to buy a house that I saw in Connecticut, right on the train line to New York City. It's a big house in a nice town where a little girl could easily walk to school, and a wife could have a big studio in the attic to paint all the X-rated pictures of Sarawak she wants."

Her hands dropped to her sides as she turned and stared at him, but he maintained his stiff pose. "I..I'm not sure I understand what you're saying," she gasped.

Finally he relaxed, letting out a huge sigh as if he, rather than she, had been the one nervously holding his breath. He wrapped his arms around her. "What I'm saying is, I don't want that hard-won reward money to go to waste. Not when I think of what I had to go through to get it!"

Drawing away from him, she put her hands on her hips, "Like scaring me half to death!"

He grinned, that rakish, lovable grin she hadn't seen nearly often enough. He pulled her against him. "No, Clothilde Jane Perkins—like falling in love with you, like getting up the nerve to come here and tell you I don't want to spend another day without you. Marry me, C.J."

She studied his jungle-hued eyes, seeing the truth behind his words, seeing the love. "Oh, yes!"

They smiled into each other's eyes. Slowly he lowered his head to hers, and their lips met.

As they touched, rediscovering their love, all thoughts of frightening jungles, murderous thieves, and priceless jade carvings retreated to the farthest recesses of their minds. Their only world was each other.

PLUS ...

For your enjoyment, here's CHAPTER 1 of

ONE O'CLOCK HUSTLE

AT 1:05 A.M. ON Sunday morning, after working twenty-four hours straight on the capture of an armed suspect in the murder of a liquor store clerk, Inspector Rebecca Mayfield sat alone at her desk in Homicide.

She was exhausted. But just as she finished writing up her notes on the tension-filled arrest, ready to head home for some much-needed sleep, the police dispatcher called: a shooting, one fatality, reported at Big Caesar's Nightclub.

Rebecca had heard of the club, located in San Francisco's touristy North Beach area. She was the first investigator to arrive at the scene, and flashed her badge at the uniformed police officer at the door. "Mayfield. Homicide."

"Good news," Officer Danzig said, all but beaming. "We're holding the killer. The bouncers caught him. He clammed up right away, but you'll find him in the manager's office."

Rebecca's eyebrows rose. She had never had witnesses capture the suspect before. "Interesting. And good; very good." Maybe she would get some sleep tonight after all.

"His name is ..." the officer pulled out his notepad and read from it, "Richard Amalfi."

Rebecca was suddenly jolted wide awake. "What did you say?"

"Richard Amalfi. He's well known at the club, apparently comes here frequently. Everyone calls him Richie."

It can't be. Her mouth went dry. "I see." There are a lot of Amalfis in this city, she told herself. "Did you see him?"

"I did. Not quite six feet, medium build, black hair, late thirties or early forties."

Damn. That sounded like the Richie Amalfi she knew. He was quite a character to be sure, but a murderer? The thought jarred her. She shook her head, needing to focus on the crime, on doing her job. "What do we know about the victim?"

"No name yet. Female, in her thirties, I'd say. We only know she was a customer. Apparently she came in with the man who killed her."

"Allegedly killed her," Rebecca automatically added.

"Allegedly," Danzig repeated. "Although they said he was caught in the act. The body's in the bookkeeper's office."

Caught in the act ... The words reverberated round and round in her head as she tried to listen to a run-down of the club's layout—the ballroom straight ahead, the coat closet and restrooms to the left, and beyond them, cordoned off with yellow tape, the corridor with the manager's office where Richie was being held, and the bookkeeper's office where the murder took place.

"Was the victim connected to the bookkeeper in some way?" she asked.

"No one has said. The bookkeeper isn't here this time of night."

Rebecca would have been shocked if he was. Nine-to-fivers liked their beauty sleep.

Danzig went on to assure her that he and his partner had immediately shut down the club and no one had been allowed to enter or leave.

She thanked the officer and stepped away from him, drawing a deep breath as she thought of all that was to come.

If Homicide were a family, Richie Amalfi would be a close relative. Rebecca's favorite co-worker, Inspector Paavo Smith, was engaged to Richie's cousin, Angelina Amalfi.

From Paavo, she knew Richie could come up with just about anything that anyone might want. Need something big, small, expensive, cheap, common, or rare? It didn't matter. Cousin Richie could provide. Many people seemed to "know a guy who knows a guy." Well, Richie was that guy—the one people went to when they needed something. She didn't want to get into what that "something" might be, or the legality of how he got it. But that didn't make him a killer ... she hoped.

She entered the elegant ballroom with white cloth-covered tables forming a semi-circle around an empty dance floor. She had never been there before—beer and pizza were her speed; jeans, turtleneck sweaters, black leather jackets, and boots her style.

The popular nightspot had been designed to look like a glamorous nightclub from the forties, the sort of place where Sinatra, Tony Bennett or Dean Martin might have sung, where women dressed in glittery gowns, men wore black or white jackets with bow ties, and "dancing cheek-to-cheek" referred to the couple's faces, not other parts of the anatomy. No hip-hop, rap or, God-forbid, country-western would ever be performed at Big Caesar's.

She could absolutely see Richie in a place like this—as absolutely as she couldn't see him killing anyone. Yet he was "caught in the act," the police officer had said.

As much as she didn't want to believe it, she needed to put aside her personal feelings. She had no more reason to believe he was innocent than she did anyone else accused of a crime. And yet ...

And yet, she couldn't help but remember the day, last Christmas Eve, when she worked alone in Homicide and he came in looking for Paavo for help with a problem. Paavo was off duty, so she ended up helping, and had spent the day and well into the night with him, finally heading home in the early hours of Christmas morning. Their time together hadn't been long, but it had been intense, including chases and shootouts, and the kind of life and death struggles—crazy though they were—that left emotions raw and defenses down. To her amazement, she had enjoyed being with him.

She then used the next several days wondering if she'd been stupid to have spent so much time with him.

Not that anything had "happened" between them. Heaven forbid! After all, from the moment she first met him, she knew he wasn't her type, and he clearly realized the same about her. Still, from time to time, she couldn't help but wonder ...

In any case, he never contacted her again—which told her that the only thing stupid was to have wasted any time whatsoever thinking about him. Of course, if he had called and asked her out, she would have refused to go. She wondered if he hadn't realized that. He was, she had discovered, curiously perceptive.

The band now jauntily played *"The Best is Yet to Come,"* but a sullen, wary mood blanketed the room.

When she left the ballroom, she found that her partner, Bill Sutter, had arrived. He was taking statements from the bouncers. Rebecca walked around to get a quick feel for the nightclub's layout and exits, both doors and windows.

Despite wanting to see and question Richie, she would save him for last.

From her several years of experience in Homicide, she knew that the more she learned about a situation the better her first questions would be, and the better she could judge the veracity of a suspect's answers. Since she knew the alleged "perp," she was going to have to be even more by-the-book in this case than she normally was.

She ducked under the yellow crime scene tape. A cop stood at the door of one of the offices.

"Homicide," Rebecca said as she put on latex gloves and entered the office. The victim lay face up in the center of the room.

She appeared to be in her early thirties and to Rebecca's eye the sort of blonde—beautiful, slim, and expensively dressed—that fit easily in a classy place like Big Caesar's; the sort of woman she could imagine Richie going out with.

A gunshot had struck her heart. Death was most likely instantaneous or close to it. Blood soaked the carpet beneath her.

Rebecca surveyed the rest of the room. The window was open wide, bringing in blustery, cold air. Piles of papers lay in a wind-tossed jumble across the desk where a brass nameplate read "Daniel Pasternak." Behind it hung a sappy Thomas Kincaid painting of little sparkling pastel-colored cottages ready-made for Disney's seven dwarfs. On the floor near the body lay a small satin handbag.

Rebecca picked it up and opened it. The bag was empty except for two twenties and a lipstick. No cell phone; no credit cards. That was surprising, and odd.

Just then, the medical examiner, Evelyn Ramirez, arrived. She wore a red sequined blouse, black silk slacks, and diamonds. Her black hair was pulled back tight and pinned up in a sleek chignon. She had obviously been called away from some big shindig and intended to return to it soon.

The ME quickly took in the body and its surroundings. "Well, this'll be fast."

Rebecca watched Ramirez do the preliminary examination to make sure no big surprises turned up—such as the corpse had actually been dead for twelve hours before someone found her, not twenty seconds like everyone said. The entry wound indicated the shot had been fired at close range, a few feet away, which was consistent with the killer and victim being together in the room.

With the exam concluded, the time had come for Rebecca to face Richie.

She took a deep breath and opened the door to the office of the nightclub manager.

Richie stood at the window, his back to her, looking into the night. His wrists were handcuffed behind him.

Two cops sat near the desk—a desk overflowing with paperwork. When Rebecca entered, they walked over to the door and stood beside it.

Richie slowly turned and faced her. Even in handcuffs he seemed calm, cool, and suave in a black jacket, white shirt, and black bow tie, almost like something out of a James Bond movie. Or, more in keeping with him and his friends, *The Godfather*.

"Richie Amalfi," she whispered.

He took a step towards her, then stopped, his deep-set, heavy-lidded brown eyes troubled and questioning. As he gazed at her, she saw something else in them, but she wasn't sure what.

She steeled herself and raised her head high, giving him a cold, icy stare.

His shoulders seemed to sag at that. "Rebecca Rulebook," he murmured, then pushed a noisy breath past his lips, and wryly shook his head. "Guess I should kiss my ass good-bye."

His saying that, his thinking that way about her, momentarily stung, but she pushed the feelings aside and concentrated on the job before her. She pulled out a chair for Richie, and then another for herself facing it. Truth be told, she moved the furniture around to give herself time to think, and to give her breathing a chance to return to normal.

"Have a seat, Richie." She prided herself on being a cop. Raised in Idaho, she had always followed the straight and narrow, and believed that all God's children were created equally. But if one of them got out of line, the full power of the law should stomp down until they saw the light. And Richie Amalfi was no exception.

"Look, Rebecca—"

"Inspector Mayfield," she said harshly, too harshly. She sat in the chair she had provided for herself and waited. She knew the rumors that he was "connected." She hadn't wanted to believe there was anything bad about him, but if he did kill someone in her city, on her watch, she didn't give a damn about those connections or family ties —current or future.

He sat facing her. "I didn't kill Meaghan Blakely." He leaned towards her as he spoke, his gaze intense, his voice earnest. "I found her body, that's all."

Thank you, she thought. He had just identified the victim. She ignored his protestation of innocence. All suspects did that.

"Tell me about Meaghan Blakely. Where does she live?"

"I don't know. I just met her." He started to stand, then changed his mind and remained seated. She could sense his tension, his need to fidget—he constantly fidgeted that one day they spent together. It drove her crazy.

Just then, Bill Sutter walked into the room.

Rebecca's partner was a burden to her. She knew from watching the other homicide inspectors that loyalty to one's partner was important, so she never complained no matter how furious he made her.

"Never-Take-A-Chance" Sutter was in his late fifties, about six feet tall, slim, with short steel gray hair, a long face, multiple bags under watery gray eyes, and thin, constantly down-turned colorless lips. He had been in Homicide so long he could have doubled as a walking, talking history book. Unfortunately, he had lost interest in the job and focused more on his retirement than his day-to-day duties. He talked about it all the time, and obsessed with worry that, like a character in a movie he once saw, he might be killed in the line of duty before his retirement day arrived. As a result, he did all he could to avoid putting himself in any danger—a difficult task when confronting killers.

Richie and Sutter eyed each other warily. Richie stiffened.

"Please continue," Rebecca said.

Squaring his shoulders as best he could with his hands cuffed, Richie stated, "I'm not saying another word until I talk to my lawyer!"

Sutter folded his arms and with a scowl faced Rebecca. "As far as I'm concerned, that does it for him. He wants to lawyer up, fine. I've got two witnesses' statements that he held the murder weapon and was trying to escape out the window when they caught him. I say we take him down to the station. If we can't question him, we book him."

A part of her wanted to believe Richie was innocent, but the evidence told her otherwise and she was too tired to try to argue against it, especially since Richie had no interest in cooperating. "You're right," she said finally.

Sutter nodded. "Good. Look, I'll handle everything. Go home, get some sleep. We've been at work non-stop since yesterday afternoon. We'll have clearer heads tomorrow."

At Sutter's mention of sleep, all the fatigue she had tried to ignore struck and the quiet throbbing of her head became an insistent drumbeat. She nodded. Without allowing herself to look back at Richie one last time, sick at heart, she left the room.

Continue with ONE O'CLOCK HUSTLE at your favorite ebook store.

ABOUT THE AUTHOR

Joanne Pence was born and raised in northern California. She has been an award-winning, *USA Today* best-selling author of mysteries for many years, but she has also written historical fiction, contemporary romance, romantic suspense, a fantasy, and supernatural suspense. All of her books are now available as ebooks, and most are also in print. Joanne hopes you'll enjoy her books, which present a variety of times, places, and reading experiences, from mysterious to thrilling, emotional to lightly humorous, as well as powerful tales of times long past.

Visit her at www.joannepence.com and be sure to sign up for Joanne's mailing list to hear about new books.

The Rebecca Mayfield Mysteries

Rebecca is a by-the-book detective, who walks the straight and narrow in her work, and in her life. Richie, on the other hand, is not at all by-the-book. But opposites can and do attract, and there are few mystery two-somes quite as opposite as Rebecca and Richie.

ONE O'CLOCK HUSTLE – North American Book Award winner in Mystery

TWO O'CLOCK HEIST

THREE O'CLOCK SÉANCE

FOUR O'CLOCK SIZZLE

FIVE O'CLOCK TWIST

SIX O'CLOCK SILENCE

Plus a Christmas Novella: The Thirteenth Santa

The Angie & Friends Food & Spirits Mysteries

Angie Amalfi and Homicide Inspector Paavo Smith are soon to be married in this latest mystery series. Crime and calories plus a new "twist" in Angie's life in the form of a ghostly family inhabiting the house she and Paavo buy, create a mystery series with a "spirited" sense of fun and adventure.

COOKING SPIRITS
ADD A PINCH OF MURDER
COOK'S BIG DAY
MURDER BY DEVIL'S FOOD
Plus a Christmas mystery-fantasy: COOK'S CURIOUS CHRISTMAS
And a cookbook: COOK'S DESSERT COOKBOOK

The early "Angie Amalfi mystery series" began when Angie first met San Francisco Homicide Inspector Paavo Smith. Here are those mysteries in the order written:

SOMETHING'S COOKING
TOO MANY COOKS
COOKING UP TROUBLE
COOKING MOST DEADLY
COOK'S NIGHT OUT
COOKS OVERBOARD
A COOK IN TIME
TO CATCH A COOK
BELL, COOK, AND CANDLE
IF COOKS COULD KILL
TWO COOKS A-KILLING
COURTING DISASTER
RED HOT MURDER
THE DA VINCI COOK

Supernatural Suspense

Ancient Echoes

Top Idaho Fiction Book Award Winner

Over two hundred years ago, a covert expedition shadowing Lewis and Clark disappeared in the wilderness of Central Idaho. Now, seven anthropology students and their professor vanish in the same area. The key to finding them lies in an ancient secret, one that men throughout history have sought to unveil.

Michael Rempart is a brilliant archeologist with a colorful and controversial career, but he is plagued by a sense of the supernatural and a spiritual intuitiveness. Joining Michael are a CIA consultant on paranormal phenomena, a washed-up local sheriff, and a former scholar of Egyptology. All must overcome their personal demons as they attempt to save the students and learn the expedition's terrible secret....

Ancient Shadows

One by one, a horror film director, a judge, and a newspaper publisher meet brutal deaths. A link exists between them, and the deaths have only begun ....

Archeologist Michael Rempart finds himself pitted against ancient demons and modern conspirators when a dying priest gives him a powerful artifact—a pearl said to have granted Genghis Khan the power, eight centuries ago, to lead his Mongol warriors across the steppes to the gates of Vienna.

The artifact has set off centuries of war and destruction as it conjures demons to play upon men's strongest ambitions and cruelest desires. Michael realizes the so-called pearl is a philosopher's stone, the prime agent of alchemy. As much as he would like to ignore the artifact, when he sees horrific deaths and experiences, first-hand, diabolical possession and affliction, he has no choice but to act, to follow a path along the Old Silk Road to a land that time forgot, and to somehow find a place that may no longer exist in the world as he knows it.

Historical, Contemporary & Fantasy Romance

Dance with a Gunfighter

Gabriella Devere wants vengeance. She grows up quickly when she witnesses the murder of her family by a gang of outlaws, and vows to make them pay for their crime. When the law won't help her, she takes matters into her own hands.

Jess McLowry left his war-torn Southern home to head West, where he hired out his gun. When he learns what happened to Gabriella's family, and what she plans, he knows a young woman like her will have no chance against the outlaws, and vows to save her the way he couldn't save his own family.

But the price of vengeance is high and Gabriella's willingness to sacrifice everything ultimately leads to the book's deadly and startling conclusion.

Willa Cather Literary Award finalist for Best Historical Novel.

The Dragon's Lady

Turn-of-the-century San Francisco comes to life in this romance of star-crossed lovers whose love is forbidden by both society and the laws of the time.

Ruth Greer, wealthy daughter of a shipping magnate, finds a young boy who has run away from his home in Chinatown—an area of gambling parlors, opium dens, and sing-song girls, as well as families trying to eke out a living. It is also home to the infamous and deadly "hatchet men" of Chinese lore.

There, Ruth meets Li Han-lin, a handsome, enigmatic leader of one such tong, and discovers he is neither as frightening cruel, or wanton as reputation would have her believe. As Ruth's fascination with the lawless area grows, she finds herself pulled deeper into its intrigue and dangers, particularly those surrounding Han-lin. But the two are from completely different worlds, and when both worlds are shattered by the Great Earthquake and Fire of 1906 that destroyed most of San Francisco, they face their ultimate test.

Seems Like Old Times

When Lee Reynolds, nationally known television news anchor, returns to the small town where she was born to sell her now-vacant childhood home, little does she expect to find that her first love has moved back to town. Nor does she expect that her feelings for him are still so strong.

Tony Santos had been a major league baseball player, but now finds his days of glory gone. He's gone back home to raise his young son as a single dad.

Both Tony and Lee have changed a lot. Yet, being with him, she finds that in her heart, it seems like old times...

The Ghost of Squire House

For decades, the home built by reclusive artist, Paul Squire, has stood empty on a windswept cliff overlooking the ocean. Those who attempted to live in the home soon fled in terror. Jennifer Barrett knows nothing of the history of the house she inherited. All she knows is she's glad for the chance to make a new life for herself.

It's Paul Squire's duty to rid his home of intruders, but something about this latest newcomer's vulnerable status ... and resemblance of someone from his past ... dulls his resolve. Jennifer would like to find a real flesh-and-blood man to liven her days and nights—someone to share her life with—but living in the artist's house, studying his paintings, she is surprised at how close she feels to him.

A compelling, prickly ghost with a tortured, guilt-ridden past, and a lonely heroine determined to start fresh, find themselves in a battle of wills and emotion in this ghostly fantasy of love, time, and chance.

Dangerous Journey

C.J. Perkins is trying to find her brother who went missing while on a Peace Corps assignment in Asia. All she knows is that the disappearance has something to do with a "White Dragon." Darius Kane, adventurer and bounty hunter, seems to be her only hope, and she practically shanghais him into helping her.

With a touch of the romantic adventure film Romancing the Stone, C.J. and Darius follow a trail that takes them through the narrow streets of Hong Kong, the backrooms of San Francisco's Chinatown, and the wild jungles of Borneo as they pursue both her brother and the White Dragon. The closer C.J. gets to them, the more danger she finds herself in—and it's not just danger of losing her life, but also of losing her heart.